PENGUIN MODERN CLASSICS
The Resignation

JAINENDRA KUMAR was born on 2 January 1905 in Kauriyaganj in Aligarh (Uttar Pradesh). He left college to join the Independence Movement in 1921, going to jail three times in the next few years. He started writing short stories around 1926 and published his first novel *Parakh* in 1929. It was followed by classics like *Sunita* (1935), *Tyagpatra* (1937), *Kalyani, Sukhda, Vyateet, Vivart, Muktibodh* (1965), *Anantar, Anamswami* and *Dashark* (1985). He also published ten volumes of short stories and an equal number of volumes of philosophical essays, most noteworthy being '*Samay aur Hum*' and '*Prastut Prashna*'. He was showered with awards and honours, including the Anuvrat Award, the Sahitya Akademi Award, the Sahitya Akademi Fellowship and the Padma Bhushan. He also represented India at the United Nations in 1979.

ROHINI CHOWDHURY was born and educated in Kolkata and writes for both adults and children. Her most recent work for adults has been the translation of *Ardhakathanak* into modern Hindi, as well as into English as *A Half Story* published as a Penguin Classic.

MRIDULA GARG, born in 1938, is a Hindi writer and columnist whose works have been widely translated. She was awarded the Vyas Samman for her novel *Kathgulab* and was awarded the Hellman-Hammet Grant for Courageous Writing by the Human Rights Watch, New York.

JAINENDRA

The Resignation

TYAGPATRA

Translated from the Hindi by Rohini Chowdhury
With an Afterword by Mridula Garg

PENGUIN BOOKS

PENGUIN BOOKS
Published by the Penguin Group
Penguin Books India Pvt. Ltd, 11 Community Centre, Panchsheel Park,
New Delhi 110 017, India
Penguin Group (USA) Inc., 375 Hudson Street, New York, New York 10014, USA
Penguin Group (Canada), 90 Eglinton Avenue East, Suite 700, Toronto, Ontario,
M4P 2Y3, Canada (a division of Pearson Penguin Canada Inc.)
Penguin Books Ltd, 80 Strand, London WC2R 0RL, England
Penguin Ireland, 25 St Stephen's Green, Dublin 2, Ireland (a division of
Penguin Books Ltd)
Penguin Group (Australia), 250 Camberwell Road, Camberwell, Victoria 3124,
Australia (a division of Pearson Australia Group Pty Ltd)
Penguin Group (NZ), 67 Apollo Drive, Rosedale, Auckland 0632, New Zealand
(a division of Pearson New Zealand Ltd)
Penguin Group (South Africa) (Pty) Ltd, 24 Sturdee Avenue, Rosebank,
Johannesburg 2196, South Africa

Penguin Books Ltd, Registered Offices: 80 Strand, London WC2R 0RL, England

First published in English by Penguin Books India 2012
Copyright © Jainendra Estate 2012
This translation copyright © Rohini Chowdhury 2012
Afterword copyright © Mridula Garg 2012

10 9 8 7 6 5 4 3 2 1

ISBN 9780143415244

Typeset in Sabon by Eleven Arts, New Delhi
Printed at Replika Press Pvt. Ltd, Sonepat

CONTENTS

TRANSLATOR'S NOTE

Indian fiction writing, as we understand the term today, came into being only in the last decades of the nineteenth century—first in Bengali, and then in other languages such as Marathi and Urdu. Modern fiction writing appeared even later in Hindi, and it was not till the early years of the twentieth century that the Hindi novel came of age.

The replacing of Persian by English as the language of the law, and in 1835, after Macaulay's (in)famous Minute on Education, the full-fledged introduction of Western education by Lord Bentinck with the purpose of 'imparting to the native population a knowledge of English literature and science through the medium of the English language' caused well-off Indians to embrace both

Western learning and English as a means of social and economic advancement. The impact of Western learning on the Indian society was profound. It opened up new vistas—of science, technology and literature. Ideas of individual freedom, human rights and democracy led to the development of a national consciousness that resented foreign rule, and gave the country a unity and an identity it had never had before. Social reform, economic issues, national pride and concern for the common man became important. Knowledge of English brought with it an exposure to English literature (and later, other Western writing in translation) so different in theme, style and tone from the literature of India. But instead of curtailing the growth and development of Indian languages, contact with English rejuvenated them—new themes, hitherto unexplored in Indian literature, came into existence. These found expression in prose, and the essay, the short story and the novel came into being.

From the beginning of the twentieth century Indian literature began increasingly to reflect the political dreams of the people. Gandhi's influence on the intellectual landscape of India was far-reaching and intense. Writers across the country were inspired by his ideas of social justice and national identity. Additionally at this time, the ideas of Karl Marx began to gain significance in Indian political thought, and to find expression in literature. Gandhi had already captured popular sentiment with his concept of *daridra-narayan*, the embodiment of the Divine in the hungry, the poor and the downtrodden. Marxist thought and Gandhian idealism combined to give rise to an intellectual outlook that was uniquely Indian, one which accommodated radical new left-leaning ideas without violent revolution. In Hindi writing, the works of Munshi Premchand came to embody this new spirit.

Premchand established 'social realism' in Hindi writing, and in 1919, with the publication of his *Sevasadan*, the Hindi novel came into its own. Deeply influenced by Gandhi, he wrote about the plight of the common man. His writings are characterized by his deep understanding of rural Indian society, his sensitive and empathetic portrayal of social concerns and his vivid characterizations. In *Sevasadan*, he tells the story of Suman—a young woman caught in an unhappy marriage—and explores issues of marriage and prostitution and Indian social attitudes towards them. In his next novel *Premashram* (1924) he takes us to Lakhanpur, a small Indian village threatened by the advances of industrialization. His vibrant depiction of the village and its inhabitants, of the conflict between the landlords and the peasants and the constant and underlying presence of a colonial government, and his analysis of rural social structure give this work an intellectual force previously absent from the Hindi novel. Premchand's greatest achievement is *Godan*—the poignant and powerful tale of Hori, a poor farmer and his struggle against poverty, caste and social prejudice. *Godan* remains a classic of Hindi literature. It was also Premchand's last novel, published in 1936, the year he died.

The vacuum left by Premchand's passing was filled instantly by his younger associate Jainendra Kumar. Jainendra had made his debut on the Hindi literary scene in 1928 with his short story *Khel*. The publication of his novels *Parakh* in 1929, *Sunita* in 1935 and *Tyagpatra* in 1937 established him firmly as one of the leading Hindi novelists of the age, and Premchand's mantle naturally fell upon his shoulders. Premchand had often presented Jainendra to his readers as his successor, and his domination of the Hindi novel and short story till the end of the 1950s more than earned him that title. However, rather than following the path laid down by Premchand, Jainendra chose to strike out on his own, exploring through his writings the inner conflicts and turmoil of the individual rather than the wider social issues that had been Premchand's concern. With Jainendra, the person became important. In *Tyagpatra* for instance, though Jainendra relates Mrinal's story within the context of contemporary society, he focuses less on the wider ills of that society than on Mrinal's struggle to live according to the norms she believes in. The wider world is, of course, always present—it is the stage upon which the play is performed—but like a stage it recedes into the background as we focus on the players and their tale.

By Jainendra's time, to the mix of Gandhian ideals and Marxist revolution had been added a third ingredient—the ideas of Sigmund Freud. The traditional Hindu attitude to sex had been further overlaid by Victorian squeamishness and Gandhian puritanism. Freud's ideas had the salutary impact of loosening inhibitions and making the exploration of sex and sexuality a valid theme in Indian writing.

Jainendra writes of such matters with a light yet effective touch. We see the thread of Mrinal's sexuality running clearly through *Tyagpatra*. Mrinal lives with her elder brother and his family, and is only a few years older than her nephew Pramod. Her love for Pramod (who is the narrator of the story) is platonic, yet we cannot miss the sensuality of her embraces, or the manner in which Pramod responds to them. One day, she returns from school, strangely restless. Pramod, who is a child at the time, struggles to make sense of her behaviour, and

That night [writes Pramod] she hugged me for a long time. She asked me, 'Pramod, do you love me?' I heard

her, but I didn't reply, only buried my
face deeper into the nest of her breast.
At this she said, 'Pramod, I love you
very much.'

Later we realize that she is in love with
her best friend Sheela's brother, a fact that
Pramod understands only dimly as a child.
Her awakening sexuality, tender and intense
and finding an echo in Pramod, is beaten
out of her by Pramod's mother; Mrinal is
then hurriedly married off to a rough and
boorish man much older than her. Later, we
meet Mrinal again, disowned by her husband,
pregnant with another man's child. She is
aware of her beauty and its impact on men,
yet matter-of-fact about it. As she explains to
a grown-up shocked and upset Pramod,

During this time of distress, three
days after I had been left there, it was
this man who, at considerable risk to

himself, had taken the trouble of asking after me. What was so dreadful about that? Perhaps he had been attracted by my beauty, but what blame could I give him for that?

She sets Pramod's fears (that she might resort to prostitution as a means of livelihood) at rest:

How can one take money from someone to whom one has given one's body? I can't understand that. I can understand the necessity of giving one's body.

Questions of love, marriage and relationships occupy much of Jainendra's writings. But his is not the zeal of the social reformer calling one to action; rather, he is content to bear witness, and to leave his readers pondering that which he enables them to glimpse.

Jainendra's contribution to Hindi literature cannot be underestimated. There was little precedent for him to follow—the novel in Hindi was too new and too untried a genre, and the psychological, a theme unexplored in Hindi writing. From Premchand's external realism, Jainendra took Hindi fiction into the realm of internal realities. He also brought a new language to Hindi fiction writing— which, though simple, is not so in the manner of Premchand's. Dealing as he does with the thoughts and emotions of individuals, Jainendra's language reflects the convoluted and complex workings of the human mind and requires the reader's full attention to follow it through to the end.

Even more than these qualities, it is the contemporary nature of his writings that makes Jainendra's work unique. Almost seventy-five years after it was written, *Tyagpatra* still finds relevance in a society that has grown infinitely more complex and layered than in Jainendra's time. Although it has been previously translated—in 1946 by S.H. Vatssyayana*—it is this relevance that made me undertake a fresh translation of *Tyagpatra*. Mrinal's struggle with social norms, her idealism, her insistence on her individualism, resonate even today with women all over the world; meanwhile universal apathy to the plight of women and the less privileged still endures.

But—enough said. The only words that can do justice to Jainendra are his own. So let us leave discussion and analysis behind, and move on to discover the poignancy and power of his writing directly as we read for ourselves Pramod's narration of Mrinal's sad but strangely inspiring story.

*S.H. Vatsyayana, *The Resignation (Tyaga-Patra)*, Benares, 1946.

PROLOGUE

Sir M. Dayal was the chief judge of this district. Resigning his judgeship, he had lived an ascetic life in Haridwar for many years. The news of his death was published two months ago. Later, a signed manuscript was found amongst his papers. One might call it a story. The abridged version of this has already appeared here and there in newspapers. This is the original document before you.

The names of people and places, and some local details not considered essential to the narrative, have been changed or shortened.

1.

. . . No, I cannot analyse vice and virtue, morality and immorality. I am a judge; so I know the limitations of the system of justice. I also understand the need for that system, for propriety in the balance of justice. Which is why I say, those who have the authority to pronounce someone a sinner, basing their verdict only on the weighing and measuring of small details—let them go about their work. I am not capable of it. That my aunt was not a sinner—who am I to say? But today, in solitude, it is for her that my heart weeps. I am secure within the strong and immovable walls of dignity and status that I have built around me. No blame or scandal can leap over those walls to reach me. But the memory of my aunt turns all my achievements to ashes. I have just received the news of her death. Now that she is gone, will that memory allow me some peace? She did not die in peace, but I knew that she would not decades before her death. Even so, I wonder whether in her last moments, she thought of this nephew of hers? To think that she might have, makes me shiver.

Our real home was towards the west of India. My father was a man of status, and my mother, an extremely competent housewife. What if she had been as kind as she was competent? But no, I will not venture down that path. If I do, I will lose my way, and my story will remain untold. It is enough to say that Ma was not as soft-hearted as she was competent. My father's sister—my Bua—was several years younger than my father but only four or five years older than me. We both lived under my mother's protective care. Her custody of us was strict, and even today I find myself weighing up the good and harm done to us by that harshly disciplined regime.

Pitaji, my father, had one brother and three sisters. His brother, at first employed in the state government as an overseer, lived in various border districts, one after another. Then suddenly, and against his wishes, he was transferred to Burma. He settled there and slowly his visits home became for him a matter of ritual only. For us too, our connection with him more or less ended. The two older sisters married and soon after died in childbirth, leaving only my youngest aunt. Pitaji was very fond of her and would fulfil her every whim. My mother was always watchful that my father's love should not spoil her; she was assiduous in her discipline. It cannot ever be said that she loved my aunt, but she did want to mould my aunt into her cherished ideal of the respectable housewife.

When I think of Bua's beauty as it was then, I am struck dumb with wonder.

Pitaji took great delight in her charming appearance. Rarely does the Creator give anyone so much beauty; when He does, He means to extract its full value at some time or the other. Anyway, let me not dwell on all that. Bua and I got along really well. She went by buggy to study in the big school in town; when she returned home, and we were alone, she would tell me of all the mischief she had been up to that day. 'We played such a trick on the teacher today, Pramod, I can't begin to tell you!' And she would burst into peals of laughter that left me gazing upon her in amazement. Reminded of the fairies I had heard of in stories, I would be drawn, enchanted, towards my aunt.

She would say, 'Pramod, you know the maths master? Sheela stuck a pin in his chair cushion, she is so wicked! You haven't seen the master's eyes, Pramod! He looks one way and his other eye looks some other way! When the pin pricked him, he was really angry. He scolded us and said, "Who did this? Stand up!" All the girls remained sitting, they were so frightened. Sheela became like a mouse in front of a cat! The master shook his cane and said, "I will beat each one of you!" Really, he was very angry. The girls saw his anger and began looking at each other accusingly. I didn't like that. I stood up and said, "I did it, Masterji." At first Masterji just looked at me. Then he said, "Come here." I went to him. He said, "Hold out your hand." I held out my hand. He struck my open palm three or four times with his cane. I had expected him to hit me many more times. But when he let go of his cane, I too took back my hand. Truly, Pramod, it didn't hurt at all. I was looking at that eye of his. Masterji was looking at me, but his eye was looking who knows where. Oh Pramod, you really must see that master sometime. Then Masterji shouted, "You won't do it again, will you?" I stood silently, thinking that now

I must play a real prank. Masterji shouted: "Go!" and I came back to my seat. Sheela sits next to me. She looked at me angrily, as though she would eat me up. I said "Silly! It was nothing!" She placed her hand over my injured hand, and holding it there on the desk, she rubbed it to stop it hurting. Her eyes were open wide. She is a crazy girl. I said, "Sheela, what are you doing? Look, that eye of Masterji's, it's looking at me!" Pramod, do you know Sheela? She is a good girl, but she is also very playful. We've become like sisters now. Sheela is silly sometimes. When I was coming home from school, she hugged me and started crying. I slapped her gently on the cheek and said, "What's the matter, Sheela? What's wrong?" She kept on sobbing but didn't say anything. Pramod, one day I'll take you to Sheela's house. Will you come?'

After relating such stories for a while, she would suddenly remember something, and become restive. She would say, 'Come on, let's go! Or your mother will get annoyed.' Bua was always apprehensive of Ma, and to me would always refer to her as 'your mother'.

Bua was not too keen on studying. But she used to keep her books very nicely and loved going to school. She was cheerful by temperament, and amiable. In front of Ma, though, she was shrinking and subdued.

Many childhood memories come back to me. How she would dress me, how gently slap me and coax me to eat, how pet me and caress me, and how she would tell me all her secrets—all this I remember.

Slowly we became older and Bua grew wiser and more discerning. I found great comfort in her presence, and hungered to be with her every moment. When she was with me, she lectured me sweetly, 'Beta, you must listen to your elders. Good boys grow up to become important men. Why Pramod, don't you want to become an important man?' Sometimes she called me Beta—

'Son'; sometimes, 'Bhaiyya'—'Brother', and sometimes, nothing at all except 'Idiot'.

I can't remember whether she was then in the ninth year of school or the tenth. I must have been twelve years old. At that time, my heart belonged completely to Bua. She loved me very much, but it was then that I realized that the nature of her love had changed. She no longer preached at me but holding me close, would gaze into the far distance. She did not talk very much either. I would ask, 'Bua, what is the matter? What happened in school today?' She would reply, 'Nothing, Bhaiyya, nothing happened in school.' And she would be unable to look at me. I would take her hand and look into her eyes and say, 'Bua, you don't tell me anything!' At this she would hold both my hands in her left hand, and slap me gently with her right hand and say, 'Isn't little Pramod silly!'

At that time, I also realized that she did not dislike solitude that much any more.

In the evenings, she would put the little *charpai* on the terrace, and lie back upon it, gazing in silence at the birds flying overhead. Sometimes she watched the kite fights in the air, and stared with fixed gaze at the kite cut loose from its string till it vanished from sight. Or sometimes she lay flat on her stomach on the charpai, and doodled on the ground with a piece of coal.

Reaching the terrace, and finding her in this mood, I would pause. She would become aware of my standing there, and say, startled, 'Arre Pramod, where were you?'

'Right here.'

'So now you don't even speak to me!'

I wouldn't reply but sit on the charpai next to her. She would gradually pull me on top of her, and say, 'Look, look at the kites!'

'Yes'.

'Do you want to fly a kite?'

'Babuji does not allow it.'

At that she would suddenly hug me and say with enthusiasm, 'You and I, we'll fly kites together. We'll fly them far and high, so high, the highest. Will you fly a kite?'

'Give me the money, I'll get one.'

She would gaze blankly at me for a while, as though she couldn't see me. She would look right through me, to look at I don't know what. Suddenly she would slacken her hold on me and, embarrassed, say, 'Never mind, let it be. Children fall and hurt themselves when flying kites.'

It was during this time that one day she was quite late returning from school. Ma asked her, 'Where were you?'

'I had gone to Sheela's house.'

On that day, Bua seemed more restless than usual. She was happy, and she couldn't concentrate on anything. She babbled and chattered about many things, flitting from topic to topic. 'Pramod, one day we should go to the bridge on the canal. Will you come?

Tell me, which sweet do you like? *Ghevar*! Is ghevar a sweet worth liking? See, you didn't get that kite, did you? Pramod, I stayed back at Sheela's. Your mother would not have minded that I did, would she? Come on, Pramod; let's not sit inside this room. Let's go up to the terrace and sit in the open. How about it?' She said one thing, and immediately forgot it. That day, nothing stayed in her heart, not thought, not its lack. It was as though her heart was filled with air, and light as a feather, wished only to fly and soar. She laughed without reason, and without reason would grab me and shake me. That day I could not understand her. I said, 'Bua, what is the matter today?'

She said, 'I'm a bua! I don't like "Bua"! Pramod you must call me "Jiji", elder sister. Sheela calls me "Jiji".'

I said, 'But for me you are my aunt.'

'I don't want to be an aunt. Bua! How dreadful! Look, see how high those birds fly. I want to be a bird.'

'A bird?'

She replied, 'Yes, a bird. She has tiny little wings. She spreads those wings and flies off wherever she wants to go. What fun, isn't it? A small little bird, with a small little tail. I want to be a bird.'

That night she hugged me for a long time. She asked me, 'Pramod, do you love me?' I heard her, but I didn't reply, only buried my face deeper into the nest of her breast. At this she said, 'Pramod, I love you very much.'

For many days after that day, she would be late returning from school. One day she was so late that the servant had to be sent looking for her, and he brought her back from Sheela's house.

It happened three days after that. I had been out and had just entered the house. I saw that Ma was snapping at everyone. She saw me and hesitated, then, her manner unreasonably angry, asked, 'You! Where were you?' Seeing Ma's frame of mind, I couldn't answer.

'Go, go fetch me the cane!'

I heard but didn't move. Then Ma shouted, 'Aren't you listening? Go fetch me the cane!'

I had no idea what had happened. I was afraid that I would be the one to be beaten. Apprehensively I fetched the cane from Babuji's room and gave it to Ma. Without a word, she turned and went back into the little room at the rear of the house. She went in and at once shut the door behind her; immediately after I heard the whistling sound of someone being caned. I stood rooted to the spot. I had heard a scream at the first stroke of the stick, but after that I did not hear any sounds of crying. The strokes were falling fast and furious. I had a doubt—it wasn't Bua being beaten, was it? The doubt would not go away nor could it be confirmed. I remained standing there helplessly. My heart was numb, and the waiting, unbearable.

After a little while, Ma opened the door and came out. Her lips were blue, her face was ashen, and the hand in which she held the cane trembled. It seemed as though she would start flaying herself with the cane any minute, and refrained from beating herself only with great effort. She passed by me and went into her own room. She stopped at the door to her room and threw the stick with great force into the courtyard. It landed near me.

I could not understand what was going on. I stood there astonished and apprehensive. After a while I plucked up my courage and entered the little room at the rear. There, lying on her face, was Bua. Her sari was awry and the clothes on her body torn with the beating. She was bruised everywhere, and bleeding too. Bua lay still and quiet. She wasn't weeping, nor was she sobbing. Her hair was dishevelled, and her forehead rested on her arms, on the ground. It became unbearable for me to stay there even for a moment. I couldn't say anything. Had I held her close, and wept, that would have been the right thing to do. But I couldn't. I tiptoed away.

After that day I did not see Bua smile again. Some five or six months after this incident she was married; it seemed as though all the arrangements had been made in a hurry. From that day Bua's schooling stopped, and she became engaged in stitching and sewing, sweeping and cleaning, and other such chores, which she did with a quiet mien. Apart from her chores, she had no interest in anything. Nor did she want to be noticed by anyone. If she wore clothes that had been freshly laundered, they would not remain fresh for long. She avoided me. It seemed to me that even Babuji's face had become sombre and heavy. Sometimes he wanted to talk to Bua, lighten her mood, make her laugh, but Bua's flat, joyless answers would make him retreat gloomily into himself. Ma was in a strange state. She scolded me for no rhyme or reason, and snapped at the servants even more. She would suddenly explode. If I were in front of her, she would turn on me and say, 'What are you staring at, Pramod? Can't you take the broom from Bua and do some sweeping yourself? Boys these days run away from work.'

Or she would say, 'Where has that Bansi gone? Isn't he here? That poor girl has to do all the work. I will fine him a rupee from his wages. These servants are growing lazier!'

Ma would say something like this every day but never anything directly to Bua.

In this fashion, the day of her wedding came closer, and she was married. Before the wedding, Bua held me close, and wept for hours. She began to instruct me, 'Bhaiyya Pramod, you must always listen to your elders. You must respect everyone. You must always tell the truth. That is how you will become a good boy. Pramod, one day you will be an important man, won't you?'

I was quite grown up by then; I wasn't a little child any more, but even so I lay quietly like a baby in Bua's embrace.

Bua said, 'Pramod, your Bua is dead, don't ever think of her again. There, what a good child you are.' That brought tears to my eyes. I did not let Bua see them but lay there, my face buried.

When Bua was leaving, I burst out crying. I did not care who saw me. I grabbed my veiled Bua's *aanchal*, and declared that without Bua I would not eat or drink; I would not. I told Ma that she was a monster and that I wouldn't set foot in that house again. At that, there and then Babuji slapped me. But I refused to get up. Her aanchal slipped from my grasp, so I wrapped myself around her feet. I held on to her toe rings with all my strength. At that, Bua bent down and lifted me up. Behind her veil, her eyes were swollen with tears. She held my chin in her hand and looking at me, she said,

'Pramod, won't you listen to me? Let me go. I will come soon.'

My insistence that I would not let her go melted before Bua's tear-stained face. I said, 'You will come soon—swear by me that you will.'

'I swear it by my Pramod.'

Ma was standing close by. Her face was pinched and drained. I wanted to fling my arms around her and cry 'Ma, Ma!' I wanted to take her chin in my hand and say 'My mother, my mother.' Bua put a silken handkerchief in my hand, and in an instant, went away. Before I could pull myself together the car had driven away from the door.

2.

After Bua left, I didn't like home any more. Ma tried to reason with me, comfort me; sometimes I would have to comfort her. After the noise and bustle of the wedding the sudden emptiness in the house seemed even more intense.

Bua came home on the fourth day after the wedding. I had seen my uncle, her husband, at the time of the wedding. He was heavily built, with a big moustache, and seemed much older than my aunt. I came to know later that this was his second marriage. My bua was like a flower. When she came home from her husband's house she brought all kinds of things for me. She took me aside and asked, 'Pramod, do you want to see what I have for you?'

I didn't much want to look at these things. What I did want was that Bua should talk to me, that she should tell me how she had fared at her husband's house, the way she used to tell me earlier of her joys and sorrows. Why was she so pale? Why did she look so dejected and out of sorts these days? Bua, I am that same Pramod, but look, I am not a child any more. Tell me what it is; I will understand your sorrow. I am not a child, Bua; I can take care of anyone who gives you grief! I don't want to look at things. Bua mine, won't you tell this Pramod the state of your heart?

Silently, wordlessly, I wanted to say all this to her. Seeing me so quiet, she asked, 'Why, won't you look at your presents? Why are you silent?'

I looked at her and softly said, 'Show me.'

Bua grew anxious. She asked, 'Why are you talking in this manner? What is wrong with you?'

'Nothing,' I replied.

21

'Then what's the matter?'

'You don't think of me the way you did before,' I replied.

Perhaps this touched Bua somewhere. She replied, 'What a thing to say! If I don't think of you the way I did before, then how do I think of you?'

'You think of me as a stranger.'

She stared at me, stunned. Pulling me on to her lap she said, 'Pramod, to tell you the truth, I am the one who has become the stranger. I am now a stranger to all of you. Your mother pushed me out and turned me into a stranger. But the place where I have been sent, Pramod, my heart does not belong there. Will you do something for me?'

I looked up at her eagerly. I wanted to tell her that I existed only to do her bidding.

'Will you?'

Hearing her ask this a second time, I sat up immediately. 'I will, Bua, at once. Tell me what it is.'

She looked at me unblinkingly for a while, then, blushing, smiled and said, 'No no, it's nothing.'

I grasped her hand and said, 'Tell me truthfully what it is, Bua. I will do it.'

'Will you go to Sheela's house?'

'I will.'

'And what will you do there?'

That confused me, and I looked at her uncertainly. She said, 'No, no, I was joking. There's nothing I need done.'

After that she insisted on showing me the things she had brought for me. One of these was a gun, which I liked very much. Bua asked, 'You like guns?'

'I will use this gun to kill crows. I don't like crows,' I replied.

Bua said, 'A gun can kill people too, Bhaiyya. That is why I have brought you only a toy. Do you know what it is to die?'

'I do. When someone dies he becomes dead.'

'If I die, what will you do?'

I didn't reply but stared at Bua fixedly. I wanted her to realize that I wasn't a child, that I understood everything. It wasn't right that Bua should joke about death. If she could die, then I could die too; I could die with great pleasure! Bua does not know just how easily I can die. She doesn't know, but the truth is that if she died, I couldn't, I wouldn't live. But as long as I am alive, we will see who can lay a finger on Bua!

The next day, Bua gave me a piece of paper and sent me to Sheela's. I knew Sheela, but I had not known that she had an older brother. I had been told to deliver the piece of paper into his hands. I liked Sheela's older brother a great deal. When I gave him the piece of paper, he forgot my presence to such an extent that I felt insulted. But then he showed me great affection, gave me a kiss, held me on his lap, carried me around on his shoulders, and gave me all kinds of things to eat. Sheela too I liked. I felt if I could find an excuse, I'd come here every day. Sheela's brother too wrote a letter and put it in my pocket. Then he asked, 'What's your name?'

'Pramod.'

'You're a good boy!' And he picked me up and gave me a kiss. Then he said, 'Give this piece of paper only to your Bua, all right?'

Had I been told to give the letter to my mother, even then I would have given it to Bua first. I didn't reply.

Sheela's brother stuffed several packets of chocolate into my coat pockets. 'You're a very good boy. Which class are you in, in school?'

'In the seventh class.'

'In the seventh class! Excellent! Pramod, tell her that I am here for a month. Do you understand?'

I understood perfectly.

'What have you understood?'

'That I am here for a month.'

Sheela's brother laughed heartily at this.

'Not you, friend—I! I am here for a month!'

The letter that he had written was not sealed in an envelope. Bua too had just given me a twist of paper. But I had liked Sheela's brother so much that I wanted to see his handwriting. I opened the letter—his letters were handsomely formed and I wondered whether I too would one day have such good handwriting. The 'My dear' with which the letter began—I liked the way it had been written so much that for a long time I tried to form the 'My dear' of my letters in the same manner. I returned home and immediately gave the letter to Bua; she opened it at once and began to read it. The letter was not long, but she kept reading it for several minutes. She even forgot that Pramod was also someone in her life and that at that moment he was with her. After a long while she lifted her eyes from the letter, folded it slowly, and looked at me—as though she did not recognize me, and had forgotten all that had been, that was and would be. She continued gazing at me with that same unseeing look; she seemed not to know who she was. Slowly she came to her senses, as though she was beginning to recognize the world again. After a little while she said, 'Pramod, now never go there again. Who asked you to bring back a reply? There is no need to bring anyone a letter. Understand?'

I had not understood a thing.

She said, 'Why can't you understand, Pramod? Don't you know that I am married?'

I replied, 'I do know.'

'You don't know a thing. You're an idiot. My heart is on fire.'

I did not answer.

'Do you know what it means when your heart is on fire?'

I really had no idea about any such passions. But at that moment, looking at Bua, seeing her fleeting smile that came in a second and vanished in the same second, the ache in my heart grew. I wanted to somehow help lighten her heart, or failing that, to throw my arms around her neck and weep.

She said, 'Pramod, if there is any message from Sheela's brother, I will jump off the roof and die. What does he think I am?'

I wanted to say that Sheela's brother had said that he was there for a month and that I had really liked him, but Bua said just then, 'Go and say so to Sheela. It is the truth; I will die. Mrinal does not take vows she does not mean to keep.'

Bua said this as though this statement was not strong enough, as if she had to convince herself even more firmly that if such a situation arose, she had to die, and was not to think of any other option.

On that visit, she was to be home for only four or five days. After that my uncle was to come and take her back with him. She did not seem enthusiastic about returning with her husband. The closer came the day when she must leave, the more fixed became her gaze. Wherever she glanced, there her gaze remained, as though she could see nothing else but Fate, and could not recognize it. She gazed with a waiting, expectant look that questioned, yet even while holding back the question, demanded an answer—'I want something. But will someone tell me what it is that I want?'

My uncle was to come the following day. That night Bua was not feeling well. She sat in her little room, on the unmade bed, and said to me, 'Pramod, tomorrow I will go away.'

I remained silent. I was massaging her head, and continued massaging it. She said, 'Now let it be.'

'But you don't take any medicines,' I protested.

She stared at me unblinkingly, and after a while, said, 'Will you do something for me, Pramod? Sheela's brother is studying medicine. I will write the name of the medicine—will you get it from him?'

Of course I would get it! She wrote a name in English on a scrap of paper and I ran off with it. But Sheela's brother was ready to beat me when he saw that piece of paper. 'What is this?' he demanded threateningly.

'Bua has asked for some medicine.'

'Medicine?'

'Yes, medicine. She has a headache.'

Sheela's brother said nothing further and paced rapidly up and down the room. The scrap of paper had been crumpled into a tight ball; he clenched it tightly in his fist. The veins of his hand stood out taut and tense, and noticing this, strange feelings arose inside me.

After a while I plucked up my courage and asked, 'Should I leave?'

Sheela's brother halted in his pacing. Looking at me, he asked humbly, 'Can I not go there and see how she is, Pramod? Will you take me with you?'

I said, 'No! Jiji will jump off the roof and die!'

At this he said nothing. I asked, 'Will you not give me the medicine?'

He replied as though challenging me, 'Medicine?'

'If you aren't giving any, should I go?'

At that he took the ball of paper that he held crumpled in his fist, and opening it, tore it into little shreds with both hands. Then, scrunching up the pieces he threw them at me and said, 'This is the medicine! Take it!'

I don't remember any event of significance after this. The next day my uncle arrived. I was not drawn to him, nor did he speak to me. Bua was very unwell, but there seemed to be nothing seriously wrong with her. Uncle arranged for all comforts to be provided during the journey, so that Bua would not face even the smallest inconvenience. Their destination was only 300 miles away and they would travel by car. If necessary they could always stop at a couple of places along the way; there were several dak bungalows on their route. Pitaji should not worry; Uncle would not let our Bua suffer any discomfort on the journey.

'All right, all right, but . . . ,' began Pitaji.

Uncle replied, 'Please do not worry at all. She will not face any problem along the way.'

'She isn't feeling that well . . .'

'It's the air and water here—a change is needed. Once September begins, I am thinking of going to Kashmir. September and October are the best months there. The air of Gulmarg is such that . . .'

The next day Uncle took Bua away with all arrangement and affection.

3.

Some time after that, we had to move towards the east of the country. I joined a school there and was moved up one class. I couldn't forget Bua. Her letters would come, but they were brief. I would learn from Ma that Bua was well and wrote nothing more in her letters. If I tried to talk to Babuji about Bua, he became silent. He was not happy and I could not understand what the matter was. I would say, 'Babuji, let me go, I'll bring Bua back.'

He would respond with enthusiasm, 'You will go?' But his enthusiasm would melt away before my eyes, and he would say, 'Where will you go? Mrinal is in her own home now. She should stay happy there. Why should it be our concern any more?'

It must have been some eight or ten months after the wedding that one day Bua arrived home with only a servant for escort. She had given us no warning of her coming. My father was displeased about this. But was he not pleased as well? Ma did not show any anger either; rather, she went so far as to curse Uncle behind his back.

Bua came home, and for me the old days returned with her. But I saw that she had become different. She was moody and unsettled; she would be happy one moment, and the next would go away and lie in the dark by herself. Her physical condition was also not good. She had become very pale, and was pregnant. She was constantly nauseated and didn't like any food. She was disinterested in everything. Alone with her I asked, 'Now you will stay here, Bua, won't you? You won't go away too quickly, will you?'

Bua replied, 'I won't go away. But why do you talk to me of such matters? Talk to me of your studies.' Her eyes filled and her voice trembled as though she would choke.

Within my own understanding, I understood I know not how much and said, 'Then, Bua, there is no need for you to go back there. I won't let you go.'

Bua said, 'And by what power will you not let me go?'

'I've said so; that's enough. I won't let you go.'

Bua gave a mocking laugh. 'You talk about stopping me, so why didn't you stop me earlier? Now nothing can be done.'

Her mood at that moment made me angry. I said vehemently, 'Why can nothing be done? Everything can be done! We'll see how Uncle takes you away!'

Bua said, 'You are very gallant, Pramod! But in this matter there is nothing to discuss with Bua. This bua does not belong here, she belongs there. Who are you to grab something that belongs to your Uncle?'

I could not understand what lay hidden behind this talk. But the distress in Bua's voice had touched me. I had understood that thinking of her husband's home caused her pain. But then, why should there be any doubt about this? If she didn't like that place, then she shouldn't go there—that's all there was to it!

But the matter wasn't as simple as I made it out to be—this I understand very well today. Marriage is not a knot that ties two people together but one that ties them to society as well. It does not break merely because one wants it to! Marriage is not a question of emotion or feelings but one of arrangement. Can it just go away because we want it to? It is a knot that, once tied, cannot be untied. It may come undone, yes, but since when has that done anyone any good?

But in class eight, I did not know all this. Which is why, at that time, with complete confidence, I assured Bua that she would

stay in this house. We'd see who Uncle was
to take her away! Don't be so disheartened,
Bua. Why do you worry? This Pramod, he
will grow up and earn lots and lots and look
after you. He won't let anything happen
to you.

I cannot say that Bua derived no reassurance
at all from my words—for, comforted, did
her face not brighten for a moment? She
laughed lightly and said, 'If you are so gallant,
Pramod, then I'll get through it. Now tell me,
are you first in your class in school or not?'

Whether I was first or last, at that moment
what I wanted to ensure was that there was
no grief or conflict left in Bua's heart. I asked,
'Tell me the truth, do you want to go there
or not?'

Bua asked, 'Should I? Tell you the
truth?'

'Yes, tell me the complete truth.'

Bua laughed and said, 'Why should I tell
you the truth?'

I became annoyed, 'You won't tell me?'

She said, 'All right, I'll tell you the truth. I want to stay with you. Will you keep me?'

She said this and looked at me in such a way that I became embarrassed, and she pulled me on to her lap. Then, suddenly hugging me tightly, she said, 'Tell me something. Do you like being caned?'

I said, 'Caned?'

She said, 'I want to cane you once—just to see how you like it.'

Bua was speaking strangely. I asked, 'What kind of talk is this, Bua?'

She said, 'I am telling you the truth, Pramod. I haven't said it to anyone else, but I am telling you. I do not like being caned. I do not like it here, and I do not like it there.'

I was astonished. 'What are you saying Bua? He beats you?'

'Yes, he beats me.'

'He beats you with a cane?'

'Yes, he beats me with a cane.'

'Why does he beat you?'

'Because I am bad; that is why he beats me.'

I could not bear to look at Bua's face at that moment. Overcome with emotion, I buried my face in her breast. My face nestled there, I began to want to hold Bua on my lap, and to pat her gently on the head and say, 'Forget all that, Bua. The good and the bad, forget it all. There *is* a place where no one is bad, and where there is no cane. That's where the two of us will live.' These thoughts in my head, I clung to her. I realized that Bua's heart had filled with despair. A few drops from her eyes fell on me.

I don't know all that happened, but some letters were exchanged between my father and my uncle. The exchange was quite protracted—Bua stayed with us for three months. Finally it was decided that Uncle could take her away. My father had perhaps agreed that henceforth if Bua came away without my uncle's permission, he would not give her sanctuary in his house. Also, my uncle had, in front of my father, levelled some accusations against my aunt, blame which he had later withdrawn with apologies.

Once, when I was with Babuji, Bua came in and silently sat down on a bed spread out on the side.

Babuji asked, 'Mrinal, tell me, how are you feeling?'

'I am well.'

'It seems as though you are not happy here.'

Mrinal was silent.

'He has written saying he will be here this Sunday. Five days. Mini, don't make this mistake again. He is a good man. It was possible to sort out matters with him. Otherwise, child, should you behave this way? A little bit of friction is always there. But a woman has no refuge except her husband's home. It is not untrue, Mrinal, that a wife's duty is towards her husband. Her home is her husband. He is her life, her duty, even her salvation. You do understand that, child.'

My father's words turned into a plea. Bua stayed silent. After a while Pitaji asked again, 'Speak, Mrinal, is there something you want to say?'

Bua replied, 'I don't feel happy. I don't want to go just now.'

'You don't want to go just now?'

Mrinal was silent—again.

'But now is when he wants to take you with him.'

Mrinal was still silent.

Babuji became a little unsettled at this silence. First he looked at me and said, 'Go Pramod; go and study.' I didn't get up at once; displeased with this he said, 'Aren't you listening? Go!' I left the room, but I did not really go away. Then Pitaji said, 'Listen to me, Mrinal. I too was not in favour of sending you back right now; you are in a delicate state of health. But you tell me, what shall I do?'

Mrinal did not say anything.

Babuji began pacing the room. For a while, he too said nothing, then asked, 'Mini, tell me the truth; what is the matter?' He said this and stood still for a while. Mrinal remained silent, so he began pacing again. He stopped suddenly and said, 'Mrinal, I can see you are troubled. If you will not tell me, how will I know? What will I do? Mini, you won't remember Pitaji, our father. You were so little when Pitaji passed away. You never knew our mother. In their stead, I was the one left behind for you. If you don't tell me, whom will you tell? Mrinal, my child, tell me the truth: what is the matter?'

Bua replied, 'There is nothing the matter, Babuji, but I don't want to go.'

'You don't want to go, that I can see—but is this realistic? And for how long will you not go?'

'I will never go.'

Babuji replied with some asperity, 'Then what will you do?'

'If you throw me out of here, then I will leave here too.'

At this Babuji became wrathful. He said, 'Where will you go?'

'Where Pitaji went, leaving me when I was so little; if anyone would show me the way, then that is where I want to go.'

After this I did not hear anything more. I did hear Pitaji pacing agitatedly across the room and, a couple of times, the sound of coughing, as when something gets stuck in the throat. I waited for a few minutes more but all I heard was the rapid thumping of Pitaji's footsteps, his cough and, sometimes, his heavy sighs. Finally I stole away from there.

When I saw Bua again, I asked, 'Bua, does Pitaji say he will send you back?'

Bua turned on me angrily, 'Be quiet, Pramod! Mind your own affairs!'

I didn't understand her anger at all. Offended, I too stayed away that day. But at dusk that day, she suddenly put her arms around me and, almost weeping, asked, 'You are hurt by what I said, Pramod?'

After a while, she herself said, 'Babuji is saying he wants to send me back. Should I go?'

What answer could I give her?

She put her hand on my shoulder and said, 'I should go away, shouldn't I, Pramod?'

Seeing me silent, she said again, 'All right, forget this. Instead tell me, if I go away, will you miss me?'

At that I replied, 'Bua, I used to miss you a lot.'

'If I die, even then will you miss me?'

I was wiser then; I replied, 'Don't say such things, Bua; I don't want to hear them.'

'All right, then tell me something—when you grow up, and I call you, will you come?'

'I will come at once.'

'In whatever state I am, you will come?'

'Yes, I will come.'

'Then listen—I say you will not come; I will not call you; all of you should forget me. The moment I leave here I am as good as dead. After this I will never bother any of you again.'

After a while, Bua asked me, 'Do you know what a husband's home is?'

I said I did not know.

'It is Paradise.'

I accepted that it was Paradise, but she was not content with my accepting this so easily. She said, 'It really is Paradise—she for whom it is not, is unfortunate.'

Seeing me silent, she continued, 'Do you know what Paradise is?'

Quickly she answered her own question, 'Paradise is a place of great luxury. It's where the gods live.'

The next morning she looked absolutely normal. She told Ma to remind the dhobi about the clothes, so that they were returned by Sunday, because she was leaving. She also asked for a few small things to be bought from the market. She appeared completely absorbed in making sure her luggage was packed properly. She would move the contents of this case into that, of that case into this. This time she would not take books; books were not good things. 'He' did not like them; they were a waste of time. No, this time, Bua did not want to take any books with her, not new ones, not any of the old ones.

She appeared absorbed in this manner till afternoon. Then she had lunch and lay down, and developed a severe headache. I asked, 'Bua, what's wrong?'

She replied, 'I have a headache.'

'Should I massage your forehead?'

'No.'

'Rub some balm?'

'No.'

'Should I put an eau de cologne compress on your forehead?'

'Arre, no no.'

I learnt that she had been constipated for the last two or three days; her stomach was as hard as a stone.

I said, 'Doctor.'

She replied, 'Everything will be all right.'

'So then what do you want to do?'

She said, 'Everything will be all right.'

Her headache increased; by late afternoon she was tossing in distress. She didn't call anyone but lay there suffering alone. Several times I rose to tell Babuji, but Bua scolded me so severely that I did not dare. Now it seemed as though she had stomach trouble. The pain would arise again and again, as though someone inside were twisting her intestines at regular intervals. The pain had made her look frightening. I don't know how I bore it all and told no one. I would get ready to tell someone, and she would make me swear by her and stop me. She would struggle to sit up saying 'May the guilt of my death be yours if you tell anyone.'

I asked, 'Then how will this be sorted?'

She replied, 'It's a stomach ache; it will cure itself. Look, when you go to the market, buy me some *jamalgota**. Will you remember—"jamalgota"? I had now become suspicious of Bua. I asked, 'What is this thing?'

Even in her pain, she laughed a little, and said, 'You are becoming wise, Pramod. It is not something that kills. You will get it, won't you?'

I asked, 'Will that make you better?'

'Yes, it will. Will you go for it?'

It is futile to describe the impact of jamalgota on her condition. My mother and my father, both became anxious. Out of fear, I did not say a word. There arose the apprehension that she might miscarry. She did

---

*A herb, the kernel of the fruit of which works as a laxative.

not miscarry, but everything else that could go wrong did. In three days her face grew so thin and sunken that it invited pity. It was as though she had died and come back to life again. A tender compassion would rise in me, but, crossing the limit, does compassion turn into anger? Full of anger, I said many harsh things to Bua. She kept listening, then said, 'You too scold me, Pramod.'

'So who else will I scold?'

'All right, scold me.'

Bua said this in such a way that my harshness suffocated within itself. I became distressed, and asked, 'So what did you do, Bua?'

'What did I do?'

'I know that all this that happened, you did it.'

At this, she stared fixedly at me for a while and said, 'Know the truth, Pramod; I didn't do anything. I have lost my mind. I can't understand anything clearly. What I do, do I know or understand it? Here there is no one to guide me. To whom do I turn, to whom can I say how I feel? Pramod, I don't understand anything. In such a situation, if even you will blame me, then what will I do?'

I didn't quite understand the meaning of her words, but my heart filled with pain. I asked, 'What is it that you want?'

'What should I want?'

'Why do you let your body suffer so?'

'I let my body suffer? I don't know. All right, tell me then, what should I do with my body?'

I was deeply distressed; my pain was without origin, without cause. I said, 'Look here, Bua, why don't you tell Babuji firmly? Why be afraid of anyone? After that I'll see who can force you.'

Bua looked at me strangely. She said, 'What should I tell him? What force? What are you talking about? Pramod, you don't know anything; you are still a child.'

Hearing her call me a child, I felt affronted and said vehemently, 'Yes, I am a child and I don't know anything. But say that you do not want to go, and I will see which Uncle takes you away! You think that I am nothing?'

I don't know why Bua became filled with apprehension at that moment. 'Fie, Bhaiyya, don't say such things! Does the female sex belong in her father's house? Have I been born different? So Bhai, you tell me, where is my father? Had he been here . . .'

Losing control, I shouted, 'What father? How you do talk, Bua! Isn't Babuji yours? Isn't Amma? Aren't I?'

Bua replied softly, 'No one is mine.'

I laid my head on her bosom and cried, 'Aren't I? Aren't I?'

She suddenly hugged me passionately, and said, 'You are, Bhaiyya, only you are. Otherwise why am I still living with this evil that is in my belly?'

On Sunday Uncle arrived. He was astonished and perplexed at Bua's appearance. He said that it seems the water of this place does not suit her at all! Just look at her condition! What had happened . . . diarrhoea? Three days of diarrhoea and vomiting? Uff! Who was the doctor? The district civil surgeon! What is this that one cannot even find a competent doctor!

Uncle was distracted with worry. His comments on Bua's condition made clear his anxiety and alarm. He said, in my presence, to Babuji, 'In this condition why did you not wire me? I would have made all the arrangements. You know how healthy the air of our place is. The food of the west is fabled, as is the vigour of the people—no matter how unwell anyone is, they feel better in no time.'

Pitaji did not quite know how to reply. He seemed to accept that it was, without a doubt, his fault. He suggested a couple of times that she was weak, and would it not be better if he waited a few days to take her away?

But the fact that she was weak made Uncle's duty even clearer. Do consider, how feasible is it to leave her here in her condition? But you will see, a few days there and she will be well again. And to tell you the truth, to worry about small ailments is to nurture them; not worrying was the medicine to beat a hundred medicines.

Uncle then said, 'You must have explained it to her—she must look after her health. And heed the world and its ways. You know this, that there are rules to govern the conduct of wives and daughters. These old traditions are what we live by. We still follow our family's code of conduct—if this is not observed, then what remains? You must explain these matters to her. I try and explain some of it to her, but you must know that your words will have a much greater impact on her.' I was only in class eight at school—at that time, what could I have understood or not understood? But even so, I did not like these statements at all, and an unfocused anger boiled up again and again in my heart. I wanted there and then to do something terrible. There was no cause for such a feeling, but the shadow on Babuji's face indicating his cowed and subdued state was irritating me intensely. I don't know what was holding me back that I did not explode.

Babuji replied respectfully, 'Ji, yes.'

Suddenly Uncle addressed me, and said, 'So tell me, sir, what's your good name? Oh, I remember—Pramod!'

So what if my name is Pramod! How does it concern anyone? I didn't say anything.

'What class are you in, in school?'

'I failed this last term.'

'You failed? That's not good news. In which year?'

I stayed silent. Why should I reply? I won't reply.

'Don't be afraid—which class do you study in?'

'I am not afraid of failing.'

He explained with great affection, 'You should be afraid of failing, Bhai. Those who put their heart into their studies, they are the ones who go on to do something in life. All right, come here. Come close to me.'

I stayed where I was; I did not budge.

Pitaji said, 'Go, Beta; go to your Uncle. Answer his questions.'

My chest thrown out, I strutted forward to stand before my uncle. He put his hands on my shoulders and gently shook me and said, 'Are you in class seven or in class eight?'

'In eight.'

'Look, you must not fail in class. All right, tell me, do you want one anna or two?' And he put his hand in his pocket.

Let me confess the evil that was in my heart. At that moment, I felt that if he wished, he could *take* two annas from me, or even four annas—what I really wanted was to find out was how it would feel to pull those big, luxuriant, pointed moustaches. And if necessary, I'd even give eight annas for this. Uncle held out two closed fists and said, 'Tell me, which one do you choose?' I stood still, staring at him, and didn't say a word.

'Tell me quickly—else the money in both fists will vanish and you will still be thinking!'

'If you want, I can give you two annas.'

He gave an embarrassed laugh, 'Ho ho ho ho!' Hearing his discomfort and the forced nature of his laugh made me proud of myself. I replied, 'I am in class eight in school and I have come first in my examinations.'

At this, Uncle laughed again, 'Ho ho ho ho!'

It seemed to me that he was unhappy with me, and I wondered why I found pleasure in his unhappiness. It felt as though I had been able to avenge Pitaji.

The following day, the preparations for
Bua and Uncle to leave began. Bua said to
me, 'Pramod, forgive anything that I might
have said to you. I wonder when I will meet
all of you again.'

I had decided that I would have to
be strong for Bua's sake, but in Bua's
presence all my strength deserted me.
Hearing Bua speak thus, I was overcome
with grief. For the sake of saying
something, I asked, 'Bua, you will keep
writing letters?'

Bua said, 'Letters. Let's see . . .'

'Please do write, Bua. When you call
me, I will come at once. I can travel alone
by train.'

'If I don't call you, then whom will I call?
But you—you'll travel alone, and come all
the way to me?'

'I will come, Bua, I will come. When you
call me, I will drop everything and come
right away.'

Bua slapped me lightly on the cheek and said, 'Silly!'

That time, as she was leaving, Bua touched Ma's feet and stood in front of her, weeping; she didn't say anything. Tearfully, Ma held her close and said, 'Mini, I will call you back soon. Look after your household well and make your husband happy, Mini.'

Ma, her voice thick with emotion, showered her with all kinds of blessings; Bua, her head bowed, submitted to it all. May you remain devoted to your husband, may you bear sons, may good fortune be yours . . . she took these and other such good wishes in a manner so submissive that it seemed she would consider herself fortunate if these wishes suffocated her to death, for if not . . . if not . . .

With Pitaji, Bua began to weep uncontrollably. Pitaji pulled out a handkerchief at once, and wiped her tears again and again. Speaking quickly, helplessly, he said, 'What is it? What is it? No no, it's all right; don't cry, don't cry . . .' Suddenly, even as he was speaking to her, he left Bua and became busy in counting and directing the stowing away of the bags and bundles and cases that were to go with her, as though he had no time; there was so much to be done.

I had sworn that I would not cry, I would not cry. I didn't cry, didn't cry. I was very angry—why was I not causing a violent upheaval of some kind? I was thinking—why does no one fight with me? I wanted to confront anyone, someone. Bua—huh! If she is leaving, let her leave. I have nothing to do with her. I have nothing to do with anyone. I will deal with everything alone. Yes, alone! Don't speak to me anyone; don't talk to me! I will not miss Bua. Why is she going away? While I am there, why is she going away? Why? And that uncle of mine, who was he, what evil, what kind of calamity, to take her away? If he was taking her away, then let him. Take her and go—at least I would be rid of him.

A groundless dread was pressing down upon me; it would not let me cry, nor let me do anything. With the result that waiting for the moment that Bua would leave I suddenly became so furious that I ran and shut myself into the tiny room that had been Bua's. Shutting the doors threw the room into darkness; I covered my eyes with both my hands and stood still and silent in the middle of the room. I hoped for a miracle, an earthquake, something, so that at the end everything would be all right. Standing there, I wanted to stop breathing, stop living, cease to exist—when I heard Ma's voice, full of emotion, calling me, 'Pramod! Pramod!'

I did not respond. I will not respond. Pramod isn't here. I don't know Pramod; I don't know anything.

'Arre Pramod! O Pramod!'

Ma's tone was such that I could not bear it. I stayed where I was and screamed, 'What is it! I don't want to know anything!'

'Where are you, child? Your Bua is calling you.'

I came out of the little room—I didn't say a word, just moved steadily towards the door. I came out and saw that everybody was ready. Uncle was saying, 'Hurry up, hurry!' Bua was standing still; her face was veiled. Was she waiting for me? I went up to her and said, 'Bua, what is it?'

She threw her arms around me and, clinging to me, began to cry in a high-pitched wail. Uncle said, 'It's time for the train. Come on, come on.'

I led her, still clinging to my shoulder, to the car. Uncle took his leave of Babuji and climbed into the car. The car growled. Uncle gave me a cheerful goodbye, 'Pramod Sahab! Your humble servant!'

4.

I will now pause—I have written enough for now. Though my heart is full of pain, I know that having begun this story I will have to complete it too. The business of living, once begun, has to be continued till Death comes to free us from it. There are no breaks in between . . . but I want to pause for a while.

So much that is happening in this world, why does it happen the way it does, why not some other way—what is the answer to this question? Whether there is an answer or not, it seems to me that all that happens has been ordained. It is not possible to rewrite even a single letter of that plan—it does not change, will not change. But the indescribable and impossible to comprehend logic of the rules . . . which great Planner has laid them down, what is His purpose—can we ask these questions and hope for answers or not?

Perhaps not. The wise have said that it is in this Creation that He is revealing his supreme wonder. I shall accept that this is so—for if I don't, how do I carry on? Nevertheless, again and again there arises in me the desire to ask Him: I grant that I do not understand Your wonders, but even so this sound of weeping and wailing that fills my ears and comes at me from every direction—what is this sound, O Lord? Amidst the playing out of Your wonders, what are these cries of pain?

The wonder is Yours, but we are the ones who live and die! Why do we live? Why do we die? Our strivings, our efforts and endeavours—what are they, why are they? We can keep asking, answer we will receive none.

Even so, the answer has always been silently explicit—it is there within, and it is evident without. Those who know can see it. Each understands it according to his own understanding—the answer is never complete. In Creation itself is contained the answer—the question is its own answer.

But let that go, all that is said; say that whatever is, is the result of past actions, of karma. I sit here on the little hill of my status which holds no meaning for me; it is false, it is momentary. My heart is not in it, nor do I feel any deep commitment to it. Yet that is what is raising me so high today. I was a well-known lawyer; now I am a judge. I sentence people to prison and the gallows, and I am respected in society. In resolution of all this, let us say that it is the result of past actions. But if you ask me the truth, my heart knows exactly what kind of karma resulted in this. In the fat corpus of a successful legal practice and this judgeship, is there even the tiniest bit of soul? I doubt it very much. I suspect that I have lost myself, which is why I have been able to become a successful lawyer and a judge. And Mrinal Bua . . . but that story I will relate in its own proper place.

I am often filled with dread. The society that gives me the esteem on which is based my high status—when I consider on whose sacrifices that society itself is based, I am repulsed and disgusted. But what can I do? What will I achieve by scraping at the foundations of that society? The foundations will become a little less firm, but nothing will be gained by that. I think all this, and do nothing.

Don't I know that all this is to fool oneself? I can climb to the top of the pile, and from my vantage point there I can bear down on society, subdue it, suppress it, but not change it. The only way to make it blossom is for me to let myself be consumed entirely by it. It is better that I should remain unknown and be true; what satisfaction is there in being untrue and famous? Ah, that kind of fame is profitless; it is barren sand that bears no fruit. If I find a kingdom but lose my soul, what have I gained? It is worse than losing a jewel and finding a pile of dust in its stead.

There are not one but many matters in life that keep whirling around in my head. If I try to ignore them, I can't. Sometimes, given the right conditions, they flare up so that in the light of their flames I see the truth. Then my judgeship appears a curse and a fraud. Truth lies in being small, in becoming a sacrifice. I have seen many things, read many things, but that is all false. The truth is only this—that he who weighed down by the burden of love experiences the essence of life, he is blessed; he who full of pride is crowing upon the peaks and summits of life's achievements, he is lost.

But why should I discuss such futile things? What is the point of such discussion? Yes, such talk relieves the ache in my heart, but when that ache lightens it becomes bearable and so definitely less impelling.

Is the progress of human life blind? It is unstoppable, yes; but that it is blind, I will not accept. Man continues along his path, while pain fills drop by drop inside him. That is the essence; that gathered pain is the jewel of man's soul, its light makes radiant the path of his progress. Else there is dense forest all around—man can find no path through it, and wanders, lost in his own delusions and petty passions, in hunger and greed and arrogance. He turns here, he turns there—but in reality he reaches nowhere. Instead, he remains caught in his own futile desires, and goes round and round in never-ending circles.

After so many years in this world, and seeing so many die and even more living as they do, if there is anything that I desire it is that inner pain should be my god, that I seek not wealth but the heart. Wealth is filth; the pain within is the nectar of the gods. Truth resides only in that pain. From the acknowledgement of that pain and all its attendant burdens will shine the light of truth that leads one towards true knowledge. All other knowledge is delusion; all other truth is conceit.

Whom do I hold accountable for all that happens? I can't blame Him, because I can't thank Him either. Why should I blame anyone? If I feel the need to blame someone, then why must I allocate that blame somewhere, why not shoulder it all myself? I should accept that our grief is His grief as well. Those who willingly and without protest shoulder this world's cruelty, and who, when it is time, lie down upon this Earth and go quietly to sleep, I salute them. I may call them unfortunates, I may even call them sinners—but I salute them.

The way that Bua died—I don't know what to think of that. I don't want anything.

Perhaps whatever happened, happened for the best. 'For the best' because now there is no way in which it can be changed. Still, perhaps I am allowed to think that the love she received from me could not in any way be forgotten, that it was pure enough in itself to open the doors of heaven for her.

But I don't know; I don't know heaven or hell, I don't understand His plan. All I know is that I was unable to ignore my heart. Had I done so, I would never have become a successful lawyer, nor had the good fortune to be given this judge's chair to occupy.

After the day when, despite the jamalgota, Bua went away with Uncle, I did not see her for ages. I moved up to class nine, passed my matriculation, entered college and even graduated with an I.A. I found new situations, made new friends, my horizons widened, and the dreams and aspirations of life reared up in front of me, their mouths agape. Bua's memory slowly faded. At first,

I would eagerly ask Ma and Pitaji for news of her—I would learn only that she was well, she was fine. I would wonder to myself what 'being well' or 'being fine' really meant. Was Bua happy? If she was happy, then was I not happy? These thoughts would rise in me, and after a while, subside. Some time later I heard that she had given birth to a stillborn baby girl, and in the process she too had nearly died. But those whose lives God saves, it is not easy for them to die. So, by God's mercy, she lived. Though 'mercy' is perhaps not the right word here, but then I can't call it the reverse either.

One day I asked Ma, 'Ma, is there any news of Bua? These holidays I will visit her.' Ma didn't say anything but stood staring at me, her eyes wide.

I asked again, insistent, 'Tell me, is there no news of Bua?'

Ma answered, casually, 'N . . . no.'

I said, 'There is news.'

'No there isn't, there isn't! Why do you pester me!'

'What is the matter? Why don't you tell me?'

'Matter? I told you, there is no "matter"! She must be well! Why aren't you concentrating on your books? It's just "Bua Bua" all the time! Your Bua is dead, all right? Don't ever talk to me of Bua again!'

I fell into confusion. 'What is it? What is it?' I cried.

'Nothing. Go and study.'

I could get nothing out of Ma; she wouldn't say anything. I asked Babuji; he too remained silent. I asked, 'Babuji, tell me the truth—is Bua dead?'

'No, of course not . . .'

'Then what is the matter?'

'Nothing at all.'

An age passed, but I could not unravel this secret. From then on, talk of Bua was forbidden in the house. If she was mentioned, everyone fell silent. Babuji's disposition had changed too—he had become grave and subdued. Ma had become increasingly irritable.

I came to know many years later—Bua's husband had left her. Bua was wicked and abandoned in her ways, and Uncle knew that she had always been that way. 'Had left her'—I did not understand right away what this meant. Where had he left her? Had she gone away herself, or had she been taken to some other, separate place, or was she still living in the same house but the marriage had ended? I came to know that he had put her up in the same town in a tiny house that was little more than a hovel. There she had to live and feed herself in whatever way she could. I also learnt that Uncle had suggested that she return home to us, but Bua had not agreed to that at all. He had threatened her, beaten her; she had been willing to die but not to come back to us. So Uncle had himself taken her away and left her in that separate house.

I heard all this like a story. At first my thoughts turned towards that story with concern; slowly, the concern became less urgent, and life, having acknowledged the story, resumed its natural course.

It's life; it carries on. No one stops for anyone—that, in fact, is the problem. If another slips and falls—well, that is not your concern, for if you stop to help him, you fall behind in the race. So keep going, carry on! While engaged in this business of carrying on I came to know, quite by chance, that Bua was no longer living in that little house. She had moved to another town—with a coal merchant. That town was not far from where we were and it seemed both strange and impossible that Bua could be living there somewhere.

Soon after this, Pitaji passed away. Ma was given to caution and avoided unnecessary ostentation; so we now began to live in a somewhat simple manner. She had high hopes for me. By this time I had finished FA, and was in the third year of college. I left for University. On my way there, as I passed the town where Bua lived and read its name on the sign at the station, a desire to see her began to form in my mind. I thought, perhaps not now, but on my way back I will definitely get off here. I will find Bua, and I will say, 'Bua! It's you! What have you done to yourself? Come with me, come away from here!'

Ma had written asking me to come home as soon as the University holidays began. The truth is Ma wanted to bring up the subject of my marriage, and this time, to finalize it. But on my way back, I could not stop myself—I alighted at that station, and located Bua.

5.

A feeling of depression overcame me as I entered that part of town. Bua did not belong here! This was where the poorer classes lived. Bua's tiny house lay deep down a narrow alley. The merchant had hired a little shop just outside, and all day long he ran his coal business from there. I hesitated at the entrance of the little hovel, then, plucking up the courage, I pushed open the door and entered.

Yes, she really was Bua. I had a moment of doubt, was that really her? It was her—dressed in a simple sari, she was making rotis over an *angithi*.

Seeing someone enter, she quickly pulled her aanchal over her head. But when she realized it was me, she remained staring in

astonishment. Did she not recognize me? Or
had she recognized me? I stood paralysed
before that gaze; at that moment I cursed
myself profoundly—why, why had I come?
That look had a quality that made me feel
that way.

A few moments later she looked away,
and, fixing her gaze on the angithi, became
absorbed in making the rotis.

Yes, it was Bua, but what had happened
to her? She had lost weight; her face was pale
and sallow. And she was pregnant. She sat
there, her body covered in a single sari, her
face shadowed by a sense of her own shame.
The hovel could not have been more than
9×10 feet square. There was a little open
space outside, where a few clothes had been
hung out to dry. Some more clothes lay in a
pile on one side of the room. Next to them
stood a couple of boxes; above these had
been suspended some bamboo poles on which
had been hung a few work garments. Behind

Bua lay a couple of half-filled tin canisters, some earthenware pots and cups, and a few tin boxes. Next to those lay some brass and aluminium utensils, and a tin bucket and an earthen pitcher filled with water. In one corner stood a half-sagging sack of coal.

I stood still staring at all this. Bua did not say a word; her gaze fixed on the angithi, she remained absorbed in making the rotis.

I said, 'I am Pramod, Bua.'

She did not respond.

I fell silent, then asked, 'Should I leave?'

But I couldn't leave; it was as though my feet were frozen on the ground.

I said suddenly, but casually, as though it was of no significance, 'All right then, I'm leaving. But I haven't eaten since yesterday and I'm hungry—that's the truth.'

I turned and made as if to leave.

Without seeming to address anyone, Bua said, 'Can you not hear; why are you standing there? Go and buy four paise's worth of curds. Oh, and get some powdered sugar as well.'

At that the man turned around and left the room at once.

I undid my shoelaces and without ceremony sat down on the pile of clothes that lay on one side of the room. I was sitting directly opposite Bua. I said, 'Bua, it's true, I haven't eaten since yesterday.'

Bua now lifted her eyes and looked at me, and said with great formality, 'Will you eat here?'

I replied, 'Bua, you may be as formal with me as you like, but I am hungry—how can I not eat?' Bua looked down again. She removed the tawa from the angithi, and put the roti that had been on the tawa directly on to the fire in the angithi. The roti puffed up. Bua did not answer but turned the roti this way and that on the fire till it was done. She picked up the roti and set it aside. Then—

I realized that it had become difficult for

her to raise her eyes quickly. I felt deeply distressed at that. I wanted to explain to her, to make her understand—*I am Pramod, Bua. Listen to me, look at me. I am that same Pramod, and you too, Bua, you too are that same Bua, are you not?*

I said, 'Bua.'

She heard me in silence.

I said, 'Babuji passed away, Bua. He carried your memory with him. Now tell me, who do I have left in this world? There's Ma, and there's you.'

Bua remained sitting still and silent; she didn't say anything at all. I wanted to prostrate myself in front of her, beg her, plead with her, to say something, anything! Why was she punishing me like this?

I said, 'I am studying for a BA, Bua. I am on my way back from the University right now. Ma is talking about my getting married. You are listening, aren't you? Ma wants to get me married this year itself. But

I don't want to. Till I finish my BA, I don't want to think of such matters. That's right, isn't it, Bua? Don't speak—but I am telling you that I don't want to get married right now. But there is no one there to plead my case to Amma. She manages to pressurize me. Bua, if I am forced into this, I promise you that I will hold you responsible—that's all I know.'

I saw that Bua's hands on the *belan* had become limp and still, and the roti on the tawa had puffed up and was about to burn.

Just then, there was a sound at the door. She gave a start and came to herself, and quickly began to roll out the roti that had been lying on the *chakla*. The man entered and put down the curds and the powdered sugar next to Bua.

Bua said, 'Sit in the shop right now, all right? Come in a little later for your meal.'

The man heard her and, staring at me, went out.

This time Bua raised her eyes and looked at me. She said, 'Come, eat.'

I said, 'First finish making the rotis; after that I will eat with you.'

Bua said, 'No, you sit down and begin.'

I asked, 'You won't eat with me?'

'No.'

'When will you eat?'

'I'll eat later.'

I said, 'When later? Why don't you eat now?'

'I will eat after I have served him his meal.'

I didn't say anything. I got up silently, took off my socks, removed my coat and hung it on the bamboo rods. I took a plate—and stood, thinking for a moment: where should I sit and how?

'Take a rug from there; spread it here close to me and sit down.'

I picked up a rug, and spread it where I had been told to and sat down upon it. As I ate, Bua asked, 'Is Ma well?'

'She is well.'

'Where are you staying here?'

'My luggage is lying in the waiting room of the station.'

'Did you come only yesterday?'

'Yes, I came yesterday.'

'Who told you about this place?'

'I found out.'

'When will you go back?'

'When you will come with me.'

Hearing this, she seemed struck by lightning. Her face went white, as though her blood had turned to ice. She lowered her gaze and did not reply. I too fell silent. After a while I asked, 'You won't come?'

Bua looked at me, still and implacable, and asked, 'Where?'

I replied, 'What do you mean "where"? Home!'

Bua, still staring at me in the same manner, asked, 'Has Ma said so?'

'I, at least, am saying so.'

She seemed to draw comfort from this. The harshness of her expression lessened, and she said, 'First get married; only after that will you have a home. And then if you come and say this to me, then it will be time for me to listen as well.'

I protested loudly, 'If my home is not mine, then whose is it?'

She looked at me silently, steadily, patiently.

I asked, 'So you won't come?'

Bua smiled a little at this. She said, 'You say that you are studying for a BA. But I see that you have still learnt nothing.'

I replied that if I hadn't learnt anything, then I hadn't, but that I was going to take her home. Bua said, 'All right, first eat. After that, do what you want to.'

I said, 'You know, I am almost twenty, I am an adult. I am the master of the house. Ma is there, but she is mine. How can I let you live here?'

Bua hesitated for a second, then said, 'If you insist on taking me with you, then listen to what I have to say—I will not go; I cannot go. You don't know me; I have left my husband's house. I have a husband but am living under the protection of another man. You may not know all this, but I do. You may shut your eyes to all this, but you cannot ask me to forget the stain and sin of my situation. And then, the man with whom I have come away, leaving my husband—how can I leave him! What has he not given up for me? I am surviving on his compassion. I could have died, but I did not. I knew that dying was wicked, it was wrong, and so I did not die. The man whose help and support saved me from the sin of dying, you ask me to leave that same man? I cannot leave him. I can be a sinner, but should I also lose all shame? Why do you harass me like this?'

I listened to her in astonishment. I had never heard Bua say anything like this before.

I realized that some inner strength of this nature must be what was sustaining her; she was otherwise half-dead in every way.

I finished eating. Bua too finished cooking. Then—

'You aren't going right now, are you? Then do one thing—the shop is just outside, go and send him in for his meal. Mind the shop for a few minutes while he eats, then come back here and rest for a while. Go once the afternoon is done.'

I went outside, and asked that man to go in for his meal. I began worrying where I should sit in a coal shop. There was a piece of sacking covered with coal-dust—I could not bring myself to sit on that; instead I began to pace up and down in front of the shop.

It was a strange part of town. Perhaps it was rarely day here—it was night during the day, and what it would be during the night, I cannot say. There were tiny hovels, stuck together; these hovels were shops during the day and sleeping chambers at night. In some were spread out cheap goods for sale, in some were laid out stale vegetables and shrivelled fruit. Here was a barber's shop, there sat a tailor sewing American-style clothes with his hand-driven sewing machine. Here the sky too becomes an alley, and time is measured in nights.

I, a BA student a dressed in trousers and a shirt and a tie, paced in front of that shop and without thinking, thought about Bua and pondered the strangeness of her situation.

Just then that man came back and said that she was calling me. I turned to go in, when he suddenly grabbed me, stopping me, and said, 'One minute, wait, just one minute!' Saying this he let go, and leaving me there he bounded off. He returned with a paan wrapped in paper; he held it out and said, 'Take this, please.'

I silently took the paan.

'Tobacco?'

I replied, 'No, thank you. I don't want anything else.'

Perhaps he did not wish me to be embarrassed. He put a hand into the pocket of his vest and pulled out a small box. He opened the box and offered it to me, 'It's Banarasi tobacco, Babu.'

'I . . .'

'It's an expensive leaf, Babu, from a special shop.'

I don't remember how much he said that tobacco cost. It must have been good tobacco. I became embarrassed at the necessity of refusing it. I said, 'Sir, I . . .'

The man laughed understandingly—'heh heh heh'—at my helpless state.

I came away. Inside, I saw that the pile of clothes had been pushed to one side, and Bua was busy spreading a fresh-looking bedspread upon layers of clothes that she had laid down to make a soft bed. She saw me enter and said, 'Come, now lie down for a while.'

I asked, 'Have you eaten?'

'I will eat now.'

'Then eat.'

'I will in a moment. Do come and sit here.'

I sat down on the bedspread. She threw two pillows towards me and said, 'Why don't you lie down?'

I replied, 'I will.'

At this, she didn't reply but began scrubbing the dirty plate left behind from his meal. Having cleaned it, she served herself in the same plate, and seeing me looking at her, gazed at me and said, 'Come, will you give me company now?'

I replied, 'You did not give me your company . . .'

'So now you cannot give me yours?'

I replied, 'I have seen it, Bua, you don't want my company.'

'I am not worthy of your company,' she replied, and picking up her plate went and sat in a corner.

She finished eating and at once began to scrub the dishes. I asked, 'Can't this be done later?'

'It'll be done in two minutes.'

I looked away and, turning over, lay there hugging the pillow. At that moment I forgot that my tomorrow would not be like this today, no matter how it would be; that in a little while, I would have to break away from this situation. I felt as though I belonged here, that I existed only to be here, and there remained nothing outside of this that was right or natural for me. My college, the discussions of marriage, Ma, my dreams and desires . . . none of that existed any more. The need for a future disappeared. What was, was all. That it was all subject to Destiny, I lost even that awareness. I did not feel there was any difference between our respective circumstances, any difference that was worth bridging through discussion, questioning, or explanations. It felt as though everything was as all right, and for the two of us to be here in this manner was a part of that 'all right'. He who is the Eternal Present without Past, Present and Future, it seemed that it was upon His directions that I, having turned into an atom of the Present, was here.

Through this stupor I heard, 'Asleep?'

I turned over and saw that Bua was sitting on the floor near a corner of my bedspread; she was asking, 'Had you fallen asleep?'

'No . . .'

'If not, then take a nap now.'

'Do you have any more work to do now?'

'Work?'

'If you have no more chores, then . . .'

'There is no dearth of chores, but we'll see about those. You . . .'

'Bua, sit here, forget about chores today.'

'I have, and I am here.'

There were many questions in my mind.

I could not fully accept that Bua herself was not responsible for the situation she was in today. Even so, even in these circumstances, there was such naturalness about Bua that I could not, in my arrogance, feel pity for her. Then what should I feel? Helplessly, I said, 'Bua.'

She said, 'Go on, why have you stopped?'

Hesitantly, I said, 'I can't understand anything. To me this place seems bad, unpleasant.'

'Who says the place is good? But it is a place. Sometimes it becomes important to just have a place. Pramod, why don't you say clearly what is bothering you?' She looked at me strangely with a look I did not like.

I said, 'You will stay here? In this place? How long will you stay here?'

'For the moment, I am here. If I don't stay in this hovel, someone else will. These hovels will remain occupied; there are many who are right for these. I don't know what my situation will be in the future. Yes, I understand that I won't be able to live here very long.'

'Where will you go?'

'Who knows!'

She continued with a small laugh, 'Do you think that this man with whom I am living will be able to support me for very long? I know that one day he will leave me and go away. That is when it will also be time for me to leave this hovel.'

The calm and natural manner in which she was saying all this was suffocating me. I asked, 'What will you do then?'

'What I will do then, do I know that right now? Can I know, even if I try to find out?'

Afraid, I asked again, 'What?'

'I won't become a prostitute, rest assured.'

I became flustered.

She continued, 'How can one take money from someone to whom one has given one's body? I can't understand that. I can understand the necessity of giving one's body. I will be able to give my body; perhaps that will be necessary. But to take in return? A woman's duty is to give, nothing else. Isn't that the ideal held up in front of a virtuous woman? She will be asked for her heart, she will also be asked for her body. But to sell that—no, no, that cannot be. If I think that . . .'

It did not feel as though she was addressing me; rather, it seemed that she wanted to silence her own imaginings with her answer. I said, 'Bua, don't get angry. But I want to know—why did you become this way? Why did you leave your husband?'

Bua looked at me steadily, 'Do you think it possible that I could ever be angry with you? I did not leave my husband. He left me. I believe in a woman's duty. I do not believe in her independence. Why should a woman devoted to her husband wish to burden him with her presence when he doesn't want her? When I understood that he did not even wish to look at me, I removed myself from his sight. He said, "I am not your husband"— after that what right had I to burden him with me? This is not the dharma of a woman who is truly devoted to her husband.'

'Bua, Bua! What are you saying? Why did all this happen?'

'Why it happened, that is exactly what I shall tell you. After I was married I thought a lot. After much reflection I reached the conclusion that I cannot deceive; deception is a sin. Whatever had happened was over; a married woman must behave towards her husband in the appropriate manner. And for that the first requisite was that she be true to him. Only then could she surrender herself completely to him. Pramod, you know Sheela's brother?'

I stared at her, taken aback at the question.

'I received a letter from him. He had written nothing special in the letter, just that he was a civil surgeon now, that he hadn't married and wouldn't; that I was married, and so he wished me happiness; and that if there was anything he could do for me, I should write. It was that letter which had set me thinking and reflecting. I wrote in reply that I was grateful for his letter, but henceforth he should not write to me and that I was trying to be happy. Before I sent my answer, I felt it necessary to mention both these letters to your Uncle. Upon hearing about the letters, he replied that there had been no need to tell him, that if this other man existed, why had I married him? A little later he said I was wicked and evil. I did not protest. From that day onwards, your Uncle began to shun me. I no longer had the right to be angry. He stopped caring about me. I deserved that—I had no right to expect his caring. I would do the chores I had to, and would eat whatever I was given and stay content within that. Despite that, I felt my presence was still hateful to him, and I could understand why. So one day, rather than continue to offend him with my presence, I went to him and told him that if he wished, he could send me away from the house. He said, "Yes, go! Go back to your own family." I said, "I have cut all ties with my family and come away from them. I can go to them when you are pleased with me, but I cannot return to them if you are angry with me—that is not my dharma." He replied that in that case I could do whatever I liked, go wherever I wanted to. I asked, "Where should I go? What should I do?" He answered, "Don't harangue me! Go away!" A few days passed. I was an impediment, an obstacle in his life. One day he suddenly cried, "Go on, get out of here!" I did not fight to disobey him. He took me to a place far away from the town and, providing me with a few necessities, left me there in a hovel. This is the whole story.'

I continued to gaze at Bua—there was no bitterness or anger in her expression. I was amazed—it was as though she had no complaint against what had happened. Thrown into great turmoil, I asked passionately, 'Why didn't you come home, Bua? Why did you come here instead with that man?'

She replied, 'Pramod, how do I explain this to you? I couldn't go home. I had gone home once and had understood then that it wasn't right for me to go home in that fashion. A woman is accepted by her own family only as long as she is accepted by her husband. When my ties with my husband broke, my ties with my own family broke automatically.'

I looked at her, perplexed. I couldn't make much sense of her words—that made me angry and irritable too.

I said, 'What are you saying? You couldn't come home! But you could come here and set up house with another man, a stranger? What kind of talk is this?'

'Yes, true, I could not go home. But I don't understand your objection to setting up house with "another" man. Besides, why is this man "another", a stranger, an outsider?'

'Why is he "another"?'

'Yes. He isn't "another". Do I behave with him as I would with "another"?'

'Is he your husband?'

'Husband! I do not know. But my existence is not for me—and yes, undoubtedly at this moment I am engaged in serving him.'

'Serving him?'

'Yes, serving him. Why not? When I was alone in that hole in which your Uncle had left me, I did not die—do you know why? I had expected and I had wanted to die—what was the point of living in that manner? But all at once I understood that He who gave me life, I could accept death on His terms as well. Who was I to choose my death according to the dictates of my own pride? If I had to die of hunger, I could, but how could I knowingly, voluntarily, kill myself? During this time of distress, three days after I had been left there, it was this man who, at considerable risk to himself, had taken the trouble of asking after me. What was so dreadful about that? Perhaps he had been attracted by my beauty, but what blame could I give him for that? He turned a blind eye to all obstacles and came to me. He had his own family, his own circle of friends and acquaintances. But he did not care—he suffered their taunts and their threats and helped me, first secretly, then openly. I had no part in his infidelity. He helped me no more than that; once in a while, he would fetch me a sack of coal, or some provisions, and say a few words of courage and support. I had already turned away from Death; and when, turning away, I resolved to look Life in the face again, this man appeared before me. Was it fair, was it just, that I should turn away from him? I accepted his help with gratitude. Pramod, you have seen him. His lust for me increased; he became intoxicated by my beauty. I felt great pity for him. Pramod, how do I explain it to you—this unfortunate man's infatuation with me grew to such an extent that I can't describe it. He forgot his family; he forgot his work; he became intent on sacrificing it all for me. One day he said to me, "Come on, let's run away." Had I counselled caution, would he have listened? Any calm advice from me would have caused an explosion—much in the way that drops of water sizzle and explode on a hot tawa! I asked the poor man, "Where should we go?" He replied, "Wherever you say! My love, you are my all!" I know exactly in what manner I was, and am, his love. He loved only himself, but he did not know that. Don't ask what the state of my heart was then—I have endured such dread many times. Even the thought of accepting his love was unbearable. But did I not owe it to him? And this also is true that at that moment, I really was his "all". If he had lost me, he would have done something terrible—he would have killed himself, or, if he had had the strength, he would have killed me. I am telling you the truth Pramod—only I know the depth of the compassion I felt for him at that moment. I have not been able to shake his belief that I am besotted with him—to do so would be cruel. Whatever little I had left, I handed over to him—it couldn't have been worth more than a thousand or twelve hundred rupees. Giving it all to him, I suggested this town and said, "It's far away; let's go there." Do you know, Pramod, why I suggested this town? Because I knew this place was close to where you live, and I was convinced that one day I would be able to see you.'

I stared at Bua; I was in complete turmoil. I did not know what I felt. This bold and resolute woman who sat there in front of me—did I despise her, or was I grateful to her? That woman was regarding me with a deep love that demanded nothing in return, and she was saying, 'But I had not dreamt that it would be you who would search for me and find me. I had thought that when I would not be able to bear it, then I would, by my own efforts, find you and look at you from a distance, and satisfy the longings of my heart. Pramod, you may hate me, but even so I am your Bua.'

I felt desperately helpless—if I could have run away I would have, but I sat there stiff and rigid, as though bound. My heart was heavy. I could not shout in anger, nor could I weep with love.

'Pramod, you see my condition, don't you? What is there to hide from you? This child that I am carrying is this man's.'

She said this, and gave me such a cold and unrelenting look that unable to stand it, I buried my face in the pillow.

'. . . you feel shame. It is a matter of shame; but I know that this man is now becoming tired of me and is thinking of his family. Even when he had been ready to leave them and was desperate to be with me, I had known that after a while he would have to return to his family, that this helpless infatuation for me would one day give rise to a mighty urge to leave me. I had known it, which is why I had come away with him. That disinterest in me has now begun. He should leave—his family is alone there. He cannot endure me forever. I want that he should continue to lose interest in me. I understand my condition—I am carrying a child. But even in this condition it is not right to think of my own interest. I will be content only after I return him to his family. The time has come for him to understand this. His obsession with me is over; he has realized that I am not his all, that I am just a vile, low-born harlot.'

I listened silently, my face still buried in the pillow. I doubt that I had ever experienced such pain. My heart twisted in anguish, and I found no relief from it. Not even a single tear came to my eye, my suffering was so great.

'I say that in a month or two, this man will leave and money will be the only thing that will matter. Which is why, whatever I can save—seven hundred, eight hundred—will come in useful in difficult times. He also knows that a shameless woman will be able to survive one way or the other, and that there is no need to leave any money with her. I know all this. Which is why I don't want to worry—except, what will happen to this child I am carrying?'

She sighed heavily; my already anguished heart trembled at that sigh.

'What will happen? That only God knows. I have no other support. But God is all-knowing and all-powerful—so why should I need any other?'

For a while, there was silence; I continued to lie there with my face buried in the pillow. Then Bua said, 'Pramod, that is why I say that as long as he is with me, he is not "another". All that I have is his. In serving him, I cannot slip in the slightest. That is what a woman's duty to her husband requires.'

After this, neither said anything for a long while. There was silence, complete silence, as though everything had come to a standstill, and Time itself had turned to stone. I don't know how much time passed. The anxiety became unbearable. At last Bua, breaking that frozen, petrified silence, said, 'Pramod, you are definitely not asleep—and here I have been carrying on, saying I don't know what. You are the one person in this world from whom I cannot hide anything. Now you rest—I will go and look in on a neighbour's child.'

I remained lying there, silent; and Bua went away.

6.

Icould not fall asleep there. I was in turmoil. How should I react to the story I had heard? I couldn't deal with it. The only solution was that I should slip away from under it and return to my own world where the value of things was fixed and where there were no complicated messes. That world where the path had been laid straight and clear and where there was no need to search for oneself, where inquiry was not necessary and a question indicated disrespect.

What do I make of this Bua? What, in this little room of hers, can I make my own? Everything is upside down here. A woman who has left her husband, and is living here in wicked adultery, talks of the duties of a wife towards her husband, while listening to her is me, a young, educated man who does not revile her, reproach her but instead finds himself drawn even more to her. Oh, this is intolerable!

This is absolutely wrong, completely wrong. I will leave; I will not stay here. Bua will not come home with me—I have seen that now. I can't take her home. Can I turn her from her path even a little? I don't know. Perhaps I can do nothing; she won't let me. Her mind works in a manner that is perverse, contrary. She doesn't want to change, so why should I try to reform her? And what's more, I began to wonder whether it was she who needed to reform, or I! This doubt was unbearable. I, a young man studying for my BA, lived in a world of lofty ideals—I looked upwards, and was filled with the importance of my ideals. I considered anything that varied even a little from those high standards to be inferior, unworthy—I didn't want to know that there could be some truth here too. And, having come to know, I didn't want to accept it, endure it. After all, I wanted to become important, great. I rose suddenly. One by one, I picked up and folded the clothes that had been used to make up my bed, and laid them in a neat pile. I wondered whether there was anything else I could do to tidy this room, but I couldn't think of anything—everything was in its proper place. Should I sweep the already clean room once more? There is no harm in that, I thought, and putting on my shoes and tying their laces, I picked up a broom and began to do just that. I couldn't find the courage to just go away quietly without further ado—after all, it is necessary to lighten the debt of one's heart, or else it feels too heavy. But I had just about finished sweeping the room, when Bua returned. I became embarrassed, and quickly threw away the broom and stood there as though I was completely innocent and had been put in the dock by mistake.

'Pramod, what are you doing? Are you leaving right now? You didn't take a nap?'

'Yes, I should leave now.'

'You should leave, yes, but the room doesn't seem so full of rubbish that it needs a broom. And why, Bhai, why must you leave now?'

'Ma has asked me to come home. I had told you—there is talk of my wedding. So I must go.'

'Talk of your wedding!'

'I told you!'

'Perhaps I didn't hear. So there is talk of your wedding. I had wanted to be there at your wedding.'

'What do you mean "had wanted"? You *will* be there.'

She replied in an embarrassed tone, 'Yes, no doubt, I will be there—my actions have been such . . . ! Has anything been finalized?'

'How can anything be finalized without me, Bua! Besides, I will not marry.'

She did not continue the discussion, and asked, 'When will you go? Right away? Does the train leave right now?'

I didn't answer her question but asked, 'Bua, you really won't come even for my wedding?'

'How will I come?'

'What do you mean "how"? You will come as one comes! I don't care about the world at all!'

'You don't care, Bhai, that can be acceptable, but I can't not care at all. I don't want to break or destroy the social norms. If those are destroyed, then what do we live within; how do we grow and prosper? Or even, within what norms shall we be destroyed? So that is why, all I can do is stay away from the world, and in its joys and hopes, break my own heart. Had I ever imagined that you would get married and I would stifle my heart and stay away from the wedding? But all right, whatever has to happen will happen.'

In the midst of all this, I had sat down on the pile of folded clothes. I said, 'So then there is no need for me to come to you either—isn't that what this means?'

Bua replied in a tone with which it was impossible to argue, 'Yes, it does mean that too, but things that are done out of necessity—sometimes their limits are crossed, and things that are completely unnecessary also happen. Isn't your coming here one of those unnecessary happenings? Yet nothing could stop it happening, and you came here, just like that . . .'

I interrupted her, 'I won't come again.'

'You should not come. I was going to explain that to you. Those who live within society also carry the responsibility of keeping its structure intact. It is their duty to ensure that only those who are the scrapings of society, or want to become its cast-offs, should have the licence to experiment with life. Pramod, it is true that Truth constantly

111

expects new directions, but only those whose lives hold no great value in society should venture or be pushed into these new directions.'

I, an undergraduate, could not understand anything of what she said. Today I remember her words, and am convinced that the knowledge we cannot find in books, we find through the torment of the spirit. What other explanation can there be for the right Bua had to understand and explain such an important life-truth with such ease? I had said to her then, 'Bua, I won't come again. I had come with a desire to help, but I see that no one takes help. That's it; I won't come again.'

Now I wonder how bereft of all sense I had become to have been able to say what I did. All that she had said in reply, I remember clearly. She had said, 'Pramod, do I not want help? Would I deny that help from you, of all people? But do you, by extending me your help, wish to lift me out of here? If that is so, then, Bhai, forgive me. I have no such desire. I want help so that my spirit can become stronger, so that when someone tramples upon me, tries to crush me, I do not get crushed but continue living with strength enough to shoulder the burden of sin as well as pray for forgiveness for everyone. Why do I need honour or status? What I need is the strength to find solace within what I receive.'

At that time I had not understood anything that she had said; in reply, I asked softly, 'Should I leave?'

She replied, 'Yes, if you must, then go and stay well, stay happy.'

As I was leaving, steeling myself, I said, 'If you need anything, please write.'

Bua laughed and replied, 'Yes, I will.'

I had stood up, had put my arms into the sleeves of my coat, and held my hat in my hands. Standing in front of her, thus ready to leave, I knew myself to be in great doubt. Let me bend and touch her feet. Yes, I must—but somehow I was not able to. Pretending that I was late, I looked at my watch and dipping my head a little, I said, 'All right, Bua. Pranam.'

And I turned around at once and walked away.

Bua said, 'Stay well, Bhaiyya.' Hearing the love and trembling in that blessing my speed increased and I didn't dare stop—for if I did, I didn't know who might hold me. Walking quickly, I stepped outside and turned at once towards the station. I passed the shop where that man, a pair of scales held up in his hand, was weighing coal for some customers. Afraid that he might see me, I lowered my eyes and quickened my steps and walked away.

7.

At home Ma asked, 'What kept you? Satish said that you had left college a day before him.'

I replied, 'I was delayed searching for Bua. She lives in that town.'

Ma asked, as though stung, 'Who?'

'Bua. I stopped to meet her on my way home.'

'WHAT?!'

'Ma, can't she come here?'

Ma replied with force, 'Listen to me, Pramod! Your Bua is now no one to us. Do not mention her name in my presence again.'

'But, Amma, listen to me,' I replied. 'I can't forget her!'

Ma replied, 'Do what you want, but don't you dare talk to me about her! She's a disgrace to our family!'

It is difficult to measure the grief that Ma felt at the mention of Bua's name; it was that deep distress which was coming through in her words. But at that time I could not understand that, and in reaction to her words distanced myself a little from her.

It is necessary to say that I could not accept the proposal of marriage that was being considered at that time. Ma was unhappy, but I had seen that I was alone in the world—no one is really with anyone and relationships are trouble.

Life continued to flow. The BA exam was near, and I wanted to do well enough to achieve a good rank. I wanted to save myself from memories of Bua—I did not want them embedded in my heart. But what was the use? Could these memories ever be erased from my heart? It is because of that memory that I considered so much of this world to be useless and worthless—Happiness seemed pointless; Sorrow seemed the essence. My dreams and ambitions seemed to dim, and that desire to compete, to excel over one's fellows, that gives an edge to life, seemed silly and laughable. But I did not want to allow myself, in this state of mind, to be swept away rudderless.

What would have happened in Bua's life? Would that man have left? What would have happened next? Huh, whatever was taking place there, what could I do about it? Nothing at all.

It was as though I had a knot in my heart, a knot that would neither untie itself, nor vanish. Rather, if I tried to do anything about it, it grew tighter, more entangled. I would feel—something should happen; I must do something; there's something wrong somewhere. But why 'something somewhere'? Everything was wrong everywhere. Creation was wrong; this world was wrong; our lives were wrong—all of this was absurd. There was no logic to it, no order, nothing. It must lead to something; there must be something that needed doing. But what? What was it that was to come of this; what was it that must be done?

I couldn't get a hold on anything, and I would bottle it all up within me; and thanks to this, I began to spend much less time with my friends. They had begun to tease me about it, but their teasing didn't have the slightest impact on me. I had not lost sight of the fact that my exam was close, that I had to do well enough in it to get a distinction, that I had to get ahead; it was just that the desire to fulfil the social demands of this world had dimmed. That ability itself had died. I did not feel that I could be lacking anything at all in life by not meeting my friends, or taking part in their laughter and jokes. I could not see that there were some things worth doing that I was not doing. One day, in this state of mind, I walked out of college and took a train to that same town in which Bua used to live.

But where was that shop selling coal? Some other people were living in that little room. I asked around but couldn't find out exactly what had happened. I learnt that that man had left some time ago, that he had beaten up his woman and had run away. But no one knew for sure what had happened to the woman after that. Yes, she lived there for about a month or so even after her man left—that much I learnt. She used to take in sewing to support herself. She was a good woman, always there with her support and encouragement in times of trouble. She would gather all the children of the neighbourhood in her house and teach them, and was always willing to help everyone with little tasks and errands. But where she went after that, no one knew.

After much questioning, I learnt that she had reached full term, that she had been worried about it and would sometimes talk of going to the hospital.

I went to the hospital and investigated. Five months ago a woman called Mrinal had come to the Mission Hospital. She had given birth to a daughter. Four days after she was born the child had caught smallpox. She had been kept in the general ward. The nurses didn't remember much—fifteen days later the baby must have been cured because after that the mother's and daughter's names did not appear in the register.

'Where did she go?'

At this, the hospital's senior doctor, a British lady, stared disbelievingly at me. She said, 'Do you seriously think that we can answer your question?'

I replied, 'Yes, perhaps you can.'

She said, 'I am surprised at you.'

I said, 'I want to know—did she want to give her child to the mission?'

She said, 'Yes, I remember now! What month was it? September? That's right; it must be that same case. How old was she?'

'About twenty-four or -five.'

'Correct. Fair-skinned?'

'Yes, she was quite fair.'

'Yes, yes, that's right. It is that same case. She had also asked us for work. She was willing to train as a nurse. She knew English as well, didn't she? She was a good girl, I remember. We said, "Give the child to the mission and believe in the teachings of Jesus Christ—then you will be able to stay here, and learn the work as well." But she didn't agree—that is the problem with Hindus. How is she related to you? Explain it to her—that Jesus is the Prophet of God. He is the one to show us the true path. We must put our faith in Him. Do you understand? You must explain it to her.'

I asked, 'What happened next? She didn't stay? She left?'

'Yes, she went away from here. I am unable to help you after that.'

I couldn't stay there for too many days—the dates for my examinations were close. I came away.

I couldn't accept this situation. I found it strange that despite all my efforts, I could not find today the Bua I had been so close to in my childhood; Bua, who used to love me so much, is perhaps hiding from me now. I would think to myself—what kind of barriers have we erected in this world that can so tear apart the love between two people? Are hearts meant to be so sundered? Are they not meant to stay with each other, together?

The question of my marriage came up again. This time, the match that had been proposed was, in Ma's consideration, excellent. It was a good alliance in terms of the family, their general reputation and character, and so on;

the girl herself was also very pretty, good-natured and educated. The delay in finalizing this lay in the necessity of my going there once, so that I could meet the girl and she could meet me. I had been putting this off for a while. I don't know why it was so, but I used to feel embarrassed about myself, ashamed. I had lost all confidence and could not think of a single praiseworthy quality in myself. I had my admirers—but I myself could not find anything within me to justify that admiration. On the contrary, that which I would find in myself made me more despondent than before.

But this time I had to go there—and as it happened it was there, in that good doctor's house, that I met Bua.

There, at the doctor's house, I realized that the young woman tutoring the little boys and girls of the family was none other than Bua. Though I did not say anything then, and she looked at me but pretended to take no notice, it was because of her that I could not stay there with ease for any length of time.

The girl did not dislike me. There was no question—as far as I can accept this matter—of my disliking her. Once I had seen her, I could not analyse her beauty or her virtues—a heavenly nymph paled in comparison to her. I had made up my mind with my first look at Rajnandini (that was her name). I had become tongue-tied with shyness; my cleverness with words deserted me. I seem to recall that I was annoyed with myself for this lack of poise. My annoyance had become somewhat evident—because it was assumed that I had not liked the girl very much. I am certain that I was successful in dispelling that misapprehension as quickly as possible.

In that household, the wish to please me increased. Everybody had been hospitable and welcoming anyway, but now there was even more reason to be so. Do not even ask me to describe my future mother-in-law's solicitude. She was constantly by my side. Casually, I asked her, 'The children do go to school, don't they, or are they taught only at home?'

She replied, 'They do go to school, but they aren't taught anything there! And here, God help us, they make such a racket! That's why we have employed a governess, as well as a tutor. I spend an extra thirty rupees a month on their studies. That is why . . .'

'Does the governess teach them well?'

'Yes, she is a good woman. She is poor, in need. But she is well-spoken and content.'

'Are the children happy with her?'

'Yes, the children are happy. Rather they are very happy. She has been with us only for two months, but she has become a great support to us.'

'She must be teaching in some school here?'

'Yes, she does. What do we pay her? Some eight to ten rupees—nothing is fixed. How can anyone get by on that? But all right, she's in need, it's some support, some help. Should I send for her?'

I replied, 'No, no. Why would you send for her?'

'It doesn't matter. Whenever there is some work, I send for her and she comes. She is alone. She helps us out with the chores—that makes her feel better, and we also get some help. She is a good girl. She doesn't take offence at anything we might say or ask of her.'

'It seems that she has become very close to your household.'

'Yes, she drops in whenever. She is very enthusiastic about this wedding. The joys of a home and a family of her own were not in her destiny. She was very eager to see you. I wonder why she went away today, and didn't stay. She must have had some work—for she was very keen to meet you.'

'To meet me?'

'Yes. She and Rajnandini have grown very fond of each other. We're all very fond of her. Wait, I'll send for her. You meet her, talk to her.'

I replied quickly, 'No, no. What is the need?'

I really did not want to discuss this further with my mother-in-law to be, but once started she couldn't stop. Despite my protest, she said, 'I will send Vithal to fetch her at once.'

I said, a little forcefully, 'Why do you want to needlessly bother someone? Let it be!'

She said, 'Bother her? Who else would ever send for her anyway?'

I asked casually, 'Why not?'

She replied, 'She is alone, a widow. She says she's from some far-off place—she has no family or kin here!'

I asked as casually as before, 'She must be living close by somewhere?'

'Just three minutes away.'

I said quickly, 'Anyway, there is no need to send for her.'

'In that case, let it be. It's true, she'll feel quite bewildered. Now rest for a while.'

I didn't want to rest, but at that moment I was grateful that she left me alone and went away.

That same day, in the evening, I went to Bua's place—she lived in a small house near the school. When I arrived there I found her embroidering a handkerchief stretched on an embroidery frame. 'Come,' she said as soon as she saw me, and getting up from her little stool, pushed it forward for me to sit on.

For a while I sat and looked at her. No one spoke. She was wearing a white sari without a border and her hair was tied back in a loose knot. The mild and gentle expression of her eyes drew one's attention at once. She held herself in a way that was both accepting and submissive, as though she had no quarrel with her Fate but rather a deep affection for it. All that she had endured, she had taken into herself so that it had become a part of her. Nothing bothered her, or caused any anguish or grief in her.

I said, 'I had gone there.'

She replied softly, 'I had known that you would.'

'I went to the hospital as well. You didn't write to me?'

'What could I have written?'

'Where is your daughter?'

'She died.'

'Died! When did she die?'

'When she was ten months old. She died partly of illness, partly of hunger.'

I fell silent. After a while, I said, 'The mission people had asked for her—why didn't you give her to them?'

'I made a mistake. But it was a mistake to have become a mother in the first place.'

I asked, 'How did you come here?'

'By chance . . . wandering.'

I couldn't ask any more questions, and

remained sitting in silence. But it did not seem to me that Bua, even now, wanted that wandering to end; she wanted to continue wandering. Fate had decreed that she was to wander forever—it seemed she knew that, and wished to accept that perpetual wandering completely and calmly, as though fulfilment existed nowhere else, she was not to look for it anywhere else.

I said, 'And now, Bua?'

She replied, 'Now, it is your wedding, isn't it?'

'Yes, it is my wedding. Had you known that this wedding was to be mine?'

'No, I hadn't. I knew that it was Rajnandini's wedding, but that it would be yours as well—had I known that, would I have remained here?'

'Why? Why would you not have remained?'

'I am an ill omen, Bhai; ill omens ruin good things happening. Why don't I go away, even now? But listen, there is one thing I will say to you—don't do anything foolish here. You came to my house this one time—that's done. But don't come here again. Does anyone know my family, where I come from, who I am? So it is not right that you should visit me. What's more, this wedding has to be done right, whatever it takes. I know the girl and like her. She is very pretty, and of an amiable disposition as well.'

I asked suddenly, 'So you think that I should accept this alliance.'

'Definitely you should.'

'All right, I will. Till now I was not sure, but now I have decided that this time I will tell them clearly and openly that you are my Bua.'

She at once covered her ears with her hands and cried, 'No, no, Bhai, never!'

I replied, 'I cannot deceive. And in the matter of marriage, I cannot deceive at all. This is a lifelong relationship—do I base it on a lie?'

Bua replied, 'The lie, Bhai, is that I have a relationship at all with you today. Tell me, what relationship do I have with you today? Once it was true that I was your Bua, but I broke that relationship with my own hands and threw it in the dust. You want to pick it out of the dust, and stubbornly call its dead and broken skeleton the truth—that is the lie. I am telling you, Pramod, leave me to my Fate. Go now, go; don't stay here any longer. If you remain here too long, it won't be right.'

At that moment, I too was truthfully feeling that it was not right for me to stay there very long. Who knows what people might think? Today I wonder why, carrying the burden of this 'what people might think' upon us, we do not walk straight; why do we walk so crooked? People have mouths; why will they not say what pleases them according to their own understanding? What is there to stop them from doing so? So why should anyone have any complaint against them? And so, for Man to take the burden of others' opinions upon himself and deny his own inner truth—how foolish of him is that?

I had now been staying at the good doctor's house for two days. Everyone could see that I knew the governess, and that my acquaintance with her was growing. In the normal course of events, no one paid it much attention. Rather, they were all so happy with her that they felt my interest in her was even a good thing. Those days passed in laughter and happiness. In a way, my worry over Bua also decreased. There were a few people to ask after her; she had enough to live on—even this little was good. Everyone was pleased with me. I had made great friends with the children, and my sisters- and brothers-in-law had begun addressing me by my new relationship with them. A few times I ran into Rajnandini—she blushed and ran away, refusing to stay a second more. The betrothal ceremony took place, and I was given the traditional gifts of money and a coconut. Even so, I was still doubtful and anxious and could not rejoice fully. Sometimes I would feel depressed that I wasn't revealing the truth. The pressure to tell the truth became so great that when the time came for me to leave, I told Doctor Sahab that the governess was my aunt—I flung the fact at him like a challenge.

He listened to me calmly, easily, and displayed no emotion other than a surprised curiosity. I told him everything and declared that he should think it over properly. I looked upon Bua as my aunt, and would continue to do so.

Doctor Sahab continued to regard me with curiosity. He said, 'But that is how it should be; what is wrong in this? I have you. What more do I want?'

I felt truly ashamed of the unnecessary conflict in me. I took my leave happily from there. Rajnandini had obliged me with a secret present and complete trust.

But the workings of Fate! The situation became tense, and despite my willingness to bend to its demands, it did not change. The engagement was broken. Rajnandini's mother was firmly against it, and the community also had objections to it. Doctor Sahab deeply regretted its breaking. He stayed in touch with me till the end. In his letters he always addressed me as his son. He expressed great dissatisfaction at Nandini's marriage to another, and I heard that there was some trouble later. Anyway, that was as it was—he could not prevail over either his wife or his community. All that happened—but then Bua was also not allowed to continue working; she had to give up the tuition. Upon hearing this news, I fell into great anxiety. I wrote to her, sent her a telegram but could not find the opportunity to go there myself—and who knows where that letter and telegram went

astray. This much I did come to know—Bua
had left that place. Where had she gone? God
knows. In this world, which place was hers
to go to? There was no such place. That is
why today every place is hers; every place is
the same.

8.

It is enough. I will now end this. Life is a story and now, in Bua's story, there remains nothing much to tell.

Events happen and, having happened, cease. We live and, living, one day we die. We start life with such enthusiasm, but on the journey across our hearts become filled with such fatigue, such confusion. I continue to ponder this strange riddle, this puzzle of life. I cannot explain it; I cannot find an answer.

There is the ocean. We have come down with our little paper boats, to sail them along its edge, but only along the shore is safety assured, for farther out it is so deep as to be fathomless. The brave do venture beyond; many drown; some can be seen swimming in the waves. But most are engaged in scrambling and fighting for a space along the shore. What else can they do? Quarrelling, squabbling with each other, within the circumference of their little circle of existence, they get ahead or lose their way, and in this manner somehow manage to live. On all three sides, the ocean shimmers and swells. Let it. We have our own concerns; our eyes are not free to glance that way.

And how can we glance that way? Upon which beach do the waves of that ocean end? Where is that coast, its farther shore? There is no shore, no coast, nothing to fix the eyes upon. There is the horizon, the line where the sky meets the sea. There a blue darkness can be seen, but the shore is not there either. The edge that we see there is the limit of our own vision and, contrarily, there too is that limitlessness at which we can only conjecture.

Oh, let us not venture there! There is no bottom; the water is fathomless. Who is there to hear you, or speak to you? All those who are, our own and others, are close to the shore. Beyond there is only reverberating silence. No, we will not go there.

We will stay on the edge, where we can touch the earth. We will venture only as far as those depths where our anchor can grasp the ocean bed and we can rest awhile. That is enough. More than that, is it not enough that once in a while we raise our eyes and look at the fathomless spread of the sea? It is enough, quite enough. Even this makes us tremble within; our hearts become afraid; our heads begin to spin, and we cannot endure it. We should look at that vastness for only as long as we can endure it, and close to the shore, live involved and entwined with everyone—this is the solution; this is human existence.

Why did Bua, both hands outstretched, venture into that fathomless deep? There was no land near to rest one's feet on. With what courage had she gone there? I stood on the shore and called to her, 'Come here, come here. I'm here; I'm your nephew; I'm Pramod, the one you love. Come here, come here. Here you will find all of us. Here there is firm ground. Here there are no difficulties. Here ease and comfort are assured; they are easily gained. There is no fear of waves; here there is dry ground.'

Bua was bobbing up and down in the water. When had she practised swimming? And into those deeps, which swimmer is bold enough to venture? A swimmer gets short of breath there. But Bua said, 'No, Pramod, no. You are my Pramod; can I ever forget that? But once the shore has been left behind, there is no going back. Even if I become weary and drown here, where is the harm in that? Ultimately are we not, all of us, destined for the belly of this very ocean? Pramod, my love to you. But you don't know—it is possible to swim only in those depths where one's feet do not touch the bottom, even if it means that one drowns there. It is inevitable that I will rise to the surface and then go under again—I know that. But having reached the limitless deep, do I return to shore again? No, such an unfortunate I will not be.'

I threw her a lifeline; she did not grasp it and laughed. She said, 'Pramod, I am very grateful to you.'

'Don't you love me? If you do, then come back,' I shouted.

Bobbing up and down, she replied, 'I love you very much; and because I do I cannot call you to me. And I most certainly cannot come to you. Look, how much of the ocean lies ahead of me. I have to cross it all.'

I cried in anger, 'Go! I will not look at you again.'

She replied, 'You should not. If you look at me too much, there is a danger of your feet slipping from the shore.'

I screamed at her, 'Go! Drown and die for all I care!'

She laughed and replied, 'It is not so easy for me even to drown and die, Bhai. I don't know how many more times I will be buffeted by the waves. But you are away and safe from those knocks—that is enough for me. I love you; that is why I say this.'

. . . the last time that I met her, I was a lawyer. Her condition was painful. She was ill, and lying in a little cell of a room. She had no medicines, no means to live. She had the sympathy of a few neighbours, but these neighbours belonged to that class of society where sympathy vanished when it came to money. I was very surprised that she had, herself, written to me. My mother had passed away; she came to know of this late but wrote to me as soon as she knew. How many times had I read that letter! I read it and reading it, become numb. I think . . . but no, I don't think, let all that be. She had written:

Pramod, to have a mother is to be fortunate. I have been deprived of one since I was born. But I regret that I could not look after her whose soul now dwells in heaven. I had hoped that I would, in her lifetime, know her forgiveness. That was not to be. Anyway, I can blame only myself for my Fate.

Pramod, you will be annoyed—so I have written my address at the top. I know that you will come. I know that you would have tried to find the place I had been staying in earlier too. Why did you send those letters and telegrams? They were pointless. Anyway, forget these matters; forget me. Life is a test—at least, that's what I have made it into. If you come, then you are welcome, but do not expect anything of me. The people amidst whom I live are the dregs of society and, who knows, maybe they are not worthy of being the dregs. But in the ultimate analysis they are human, a fact I see clearly now that I find myself amongst them. I no longer want any other support to live, except their dimming and awakening humanity. I have wandered far and wide, and suffered much; I have learnt that the good wishes of poor people are my only wealth. I have no desire left now to live for any other reason—that is how I feel. In these people, whom we call inferior, there are many layers; beneath these layers there remains one from which, if we could but touch it, there bursts forth the dormant quality of goodness, pure as milk. It is no longer difficult for me to understand the notion that God resides in everyone, and that He is omnipresent. And so, I don't want to break from this and uproot myself. Why should I want to? How is it different anywhere?

What's the benefit of this place, you will ask. There is great benefit—here no one has the desire to say that he is a virtuous man. Here, the worth of a man is not measured in terms of his virtue or good character but rather by his wretchedness; it is by that reckoning that a man's value rises or falls. I agree that this is the root of evil; there is frightening apathy and dullness of intellect here. But it is also beneficial. In this place, it is inconceivable that anyone would present himself as being of good character, or that he would wish to or be able to do so. Here virtue has no value; it is not held in any esteem. Rather, its lack has value. If, inside one, even as deep inside as the pith, there lies hidden the germ of joy, here it will rise to the surface. Here pretence and deceit are impossible, but they are so necessary in genteel society.

Here refinement is not a requirement; good breeding is not expected. The more the shamelessness—no matter how dissipated and dissolute—that is revealed, the more sensuous it becomes; crudeness and barbarity do not need the shield of modesty. Yes, a man can turn into an animal and do so with pride; and those who can't are considered deficient as men. This is why someone who demonstrates virtue cannot survive here. He will have to be true down to his very essence; only then will he be safe. That which is without must be within. If there be an animal within, then in this environment the surface humanity will not last a second. If he be a man, then he will be a man right through. Good breeding that is only a veneer is revealed here for what it is. Only pure gold can survive here, because it does not need to declare that it is not bronze. Here there is no demand for gold, nor any bias against bronze. So the desire to look like gold while being bronze within will not survive here for a second; rather bronze is valued here. The constancy of gold is tested here—the true test of real gold is here. This place is the touchstone. I believe that he who is revealed as genuine on this touchstone, he is true. And only he can be beloved of God.

Pramod, you will not understand, but it is best that you do not come here. You are sweet-natured and gentle; you think high thoughts. Here there is no gentleness, no high thinking, but filth and brute dullness. I manage to breathe and survive amongst them, because I have become used to them. Perhaps the softer, loftier functions of my mind have become dulled. But it is better that you do not come—to lose your love will

be unbearable for me. Today I know
no one, except you, who belongs to
genteel society; nor does anyone know
me. But it is because of you alone that
I have been saved from disliking that
entire worthy strata of society. Pramod,
you do not know how big a favour you
are unwittingly doing my soul. The
community of which you are a part—
can I ever bring myself to revile that as
long as you are in it? Sometimes I feel
a great contempt for it, but I remember
your love and become weak, and my
heart's bitterness cannot destroy my
well-being. Bitterness arises in me, but
my memories of you help me turn that
very bitterness into the strength that
nourishes me, sustains me. Your love
keeps me in good health, but I am afraid
that should you come here I may lose
what remains to me of your love! Then
what will become of me? Living will

become a trial; I will lose my strength. How will faith be sustained? Then the filth will surround me and overwhelm me. How will I continue without the one support of my life? Now I can lift high my spirit and, filling my lungs with clean air, continue to live with ease in this poisonous atmosphere. If your love no longer remains, how will I carry on? I am not afraid that I may die but that I may lose the very prop of my life; that is a great fear. As long as faith remains, it is acceptable even to die, but if faith is lost, what will I have left? And so I say, stay away. Now don't come where I am; for the reasons I have given you, the place where I am is not fit for you to see. And because of you, though I live here, I am still not of here. Do not come; do not. If you come, on your head be it.

How I have ended up writing such a long letter, and why, I do not know. But

I do know that I could not have written all this to anyone but you; and had I even thought of these matters, I could not have understood them.

Pramod, do not think it impossible that I may call you and say 'save me, deliver me'. When my faith within breaks, I will call you. But do not come to me on these words of mine; do not come to me now—this I request of you.

But I want to conclude this account. Why should I extend it needlessly? It distresses me to describe the place and condition in which I found Bua; I will not give a description. It is not possible to guess even a little at her state from this letter of Bua's. She lived where the filth of the city lives—that place was the abode of prostitutes past their prime, unemployed labourers, professional beggars, criminals who had escaped and were wanted by the law for their secret and perverse activities. How did Bua end up there? She was ill, and bound to her bed. Four or five of the sort of men and women I have described above were about her; their faces showed concern and worry about Bua's condition. They seemed troubled, but their manner of speaking was very casual, and the frankness of their speech made me feel nauseated. Even though their respect for Bua was evident, they used the familiar form of address for everyone. There was no shame or modesty there and, even around Bua's sickbed, they could not refrain from obscene gestures amongst themselves. They showed no happiness at finding me, a stranger, amongst them. It was as though I was some alien creature, unbelievable, frightening. Many of them were certain that I was a former lover of their acquaintance's, the sick woman lying upon her bed, and that I was responsible for her condition. They expressed these suspicions so openly that

I cringed within myself and could not say a word.

Bua listened to it all and bore it with fortitude. Sometimes she would even reprimand someone's vulgarity, and her rebuke would even have some effect, but more often she would remain indifferent to that aspect.

I said, 'Bua, now come. I have come to take you.'

'Where will you take me?'

'Now the house is mine alone, Bua! I am married, and it is my authority that prevails; there is no third person there. Come, now it will be your rule.'

'You want me to come—in this old age?'

'Yes, yes. It is in old age that you must come. If I cannot give you comfort in old age, then when will I? I won't listen to anything more. I promise you that my law practice will do well. There are no worries, Bua, the officials are my friends. I don't give a damn about anyone.'

Bua listened in silence, then said, 'Pramod, you have read the Mahabharata—when Yudhishthir went to Heaven, he did not leave the dog behind. Tell me, how big is your house—will you be able to take all these people as well? They are not dogs, and they have done much for me; I owe them a great deal.'

I stopped her at once, 'You do say strange things, Bua! Am I no one at all? We will see how I will not take you with me!'

Bua smiled calmly at me and said, 'When do I ever refuse? All right, you will assuredly take me away.'

'I will most certainly.'

'Listen. You will assuredly take me away?'

'Yes, yes—I am saying so, am I not? I will assuredly take you away.'

Bua said, 'Then tell me this—do you have a lot of money? How much?'

'Money?'

153

She said, 'Leave behind whatever you can spare. Then it will be the same as though I had gone home with you, will it not? What do you say to that?'

I stared at her in astonishment. For the sake of saying something, I asked, 'What will you do with the money?'

'What will I do with it—that I don't know yet. But first it will clear the misapprehension in your heart that I do want your help. And then, it is good for you too to leave some money behind—earn well, and throw your earnings into this hole. Do you hear me? I don't know if money can turn this hellhole into heaven, but some use can always be found for it.'

I didn't understand this at all. I put it aside and said, 'Come, let me admit you to the hospital here.'

She said, 'You didn't understand what I said, did you? All right, never mind. No Bhai, why should I go to the hospital?'

'You will be well-looked after in a hospital. I will arrange a private ward for you—don't worry about expenses, Bua.'

Bua interrupted, 'But that is precisely my worry, Pramod! Even if you leave behind a lot of money, I am not about to run to the private ward of the hospital. Pramod, as long as this body exists, so will a dozen illnesses and infirmities. So why the worry and anxiety?'

Why prolong this further? The details will only serve to highlight my cowardice. The main point is that I could not bring her back with me. I cannot even say that I was able to make any special arrangements for her food and medicines. I had given a couple of hundred rupees to a local lawyer whom I knew, and asked him to keep an eye on Bua. He must have kept an eye on her, and even spent that money on her, but I am certain the looking after and the spending must have been done only when absolutely necessary.

The result was that I, offended and angry, reproached and reprimanded her, and after many emphatic instructions and reproofs, went away.

I came back and did not go there again. I immersed myself so deeply in my legal practice that I did not raise my eyes to look at anything else, saw nothing else. I looked at my own interests and aims and . . . and that was enough.

But why? Why could I not fulfil Bua's request? She loved me so much, trusted me so much—so when she asked me a question, why could I not, in answer, lay my wealth before her? Why did I clench my fist shut? And even if this did happen, then why, after, did my soul not writhe in anguish? Why? The question is—Why?

I will now answer this 'Why?' The answer is that I was small and contemptible. Why did I bury myself in my practice bent on forgetting? Why did I insist on believing that

I was right? Why did I keep on ignoring what I had to do and continue doing that which was not important? The answer is that I was sensible, but I was not sincere. I weighed everything along my path, and always kept the scales in my own hands.

That is why, today, being weighed on the scales that matter, I am found wanting. Today I sit atop the riches and accomplishment of my legal practice and think—why could I not become a little sincere, a little ordinary? What should I now do with all this when I could not give back love a gift in return when there was still time? All this that I have gathered is dirt, dirt which is covering the light of my soul. I don't want all this . . .

Some seventeen years or more have passed since that incident. Today the issue that deeply astonishes and greatly torments me is this: what inhumanity enabled me to live for seventeen years without seeing Bua? That Bua, who gave without ever taking; who, if she was guilty of anything, was guilty of loving me; whose memory now burns within me like a red-hot ember. Her life, whatever it might have been, always glowed clear like a rising flame; if there was smoke, no matter, for the flame was always bright. How was I able to push Bua aside and continue to deceive myself?

Today the news has come that she is dead. How she died—there is no need to know. What I already know, that is more than enough. If I can understand even that much, I will become a different man.

Bua, you have gone. While you were alive, I did not mend my ways. Now listen, I give up this judgeship. I will give up all worldly concerns entirely. I may not be able to learn afresh to live for others—my habits are set, but for myself I will live with only the little that is absolutely necessary to stay alive. I promise you this.

Dear God, You can hear what I have said. Even if you do not send me to Hell otherwise, send me there if I break my promise.

(Signed) M. Dayal
Dt. 3/4

(*Later*) With this I affirm that I have given in my resignation from the judgeship.

M.D.
Dt. 4/4

THE CRAFTING OF SILENCE

Yet I say, save literature from restraint.
Save it for if you are ever in need of
restraint over yourself, you shall find it
nowhere but in literature.
—Jainendra, 1970

Jainendra Kumar, the little master of
Hindi literature, passed away in silence
on 4 December 1988 after fifty-eight years
of creative writing and eighty-three of
reflective living. He had passed into silence
in 1986, when a paralytic stroke claimed
his voice. His voice was his pen. So it was
more than a voice which was stilled; it was
the muse itself. Jainendra was one of the few
writers who dictated rather than penned his
formidable body of work: thirteen novels and

a vast number of short stories and essays. I am convinced that the extreme economy of words, a distinctive hallmark of his style, was partly due to the fact that he spoke rather than wrote them.

It is easy for a painter or a sculptor to portray silence on his canvas or medium. A musician or a dancer can conjure silence in the abstraction of the notes and beats. But a writer is doomed to use words—his only tool. How does he then craft silence the way Jainendra did by using them so that they mean more when they are not spoken than when they are? He perfected the art of silence to a degree unmatched by any Hindi writer before or since. Restraint was the essence of his craft and the philosophy underlying it. One can say it was the very essence of Jainendra.

When I read his novels, I am reminded of my grandmother's chulha. The glow, the cackle, the hiss, the silent smouldering, with the wood fire dying so slowly and operatically that you felt you were watching an elaborate and sacred ritual. His language had all the qualities of old-fashioned wood fire—the painstakingly collected and economically built. But old-fashioned, Jainendra was not! He broke every rule of grammar and syntax, juggled verbs, threw out every superfluous word to craft a new language suited to restraint, renunciation and silence, essential to his creativity and world view. His distinction and inimitability lay in the way he used chaste khadi boli, without simplifying it. It was unalloyed with Urdu or regional dialect, yet a language only he could write, free from the dictates of grammar as practised by his peers, contemporaries and future generations. Its essence lay in its being closer to the spoken than the written word: simple yet mystical, silent yet vibrating with layer upon layer of meaning. He perfected restraint to make the language vibrate in the flow of words as much as in their lack, perhaps more so. This crafting of renunciation made it impossible to separate the form from the content in his works; one flowed from the other and merged with it as surely as the atman merges with the paramatman.

Tyagpatra, the novel translated here as *The Resignation* by Rohini Chowdhury and first translated by S.H. Vatsyayana 'Agyeya' in 1946 under the same title, is perhaps Jainendra's most quoted and translated work. Interestingly, it is called *Tyag-patra* in German. According to Jainendra, when he was asked to choose from a number of German equivalents, he asked innocuously, 'Would you translate my name also?' The thrust went home and both his name and the original Hindi title of the novel were retained.

The Hindi reader was not ready either when Jainendra first made his onslaught on khadi boli, exchanging mystique for syntax with the minimum expenditure of words. The modern Hindi writer owes a debt to him for clearing the way for spirited experimentation with language, rejecting verbosity and deliberate use of dialect. In any case, since he did not believe in the depiction of factual reality but its transcendence to portray a state of mind, he did not need local dialects.

It is significant that as the obsession for using literary characters to unfold a philosophy took greater hold of him, his women characters gradually changed from unusual to improbable, since they were the ones used as the medium for the revelation of this philosophy. He also lost his command over silence and started playing with words. Ultimately he gave up his awesome brevity for discourse. The trend started with *Muktibodh* (1965), the Sahitya Akademi Award winner, and culminated in his last novel, *Dashark* (1985).

To fully understand his novels, it is vital to examine the philosophy which served as their launching pad. The essential ingredients were restraint, renunciation, love and freedom of choice. In *Tyagpatra,* Mrinal, a vivacious young girl is thrown in a marriage which snatches every vestige of respectability and individuality from her. As a newly-wed, she confides a premarital feeling of love for a youth—a feeling, no more—to her husband, only to find that he gave a fig for honesty or truthfulness. Cast away by him, she lives with a lowly, uncouth and violent coal-seller and gets pregnant. After her child dies, she shifts to the slums to serve the outcasts and rejects of society. When her well-heeled nephew, a judge, comes to take her home with him, she spurns him, saying, '. . . when Yudhisthir went to Heaven he did not leave the dog behind. Tell me, how big is your house—will you be able to take all these people as well? They are not

dogs, and they have done much for me . . .'
When he insists, she asks him to leave his
money for the slum-dwellers. He does not.
It is only after she dies that he wakes up to
the futility of the material world and resigns
from his post.

That is the fate of almost all the men in
Jainendra's novels: cruelty, failure and a
late renunciation. What comes easily and
with charm to women makes men inactive
and cruel towards women. They opt for
renunciation after a good deal of self-analysis
and philosophical dilemma. Even when they
don't, as in *Muktibodh*, the state of mind
is that of an ascetic, not that of a man of
action. Unfortunately this karma without
desire is born of inertia, lassitude and an
unrepentant use of women rather than
intuitive renunciation.

Significantly most of the men in his novels
are well heeled: lawyers, judges, members of
parliament, ministers, and so on. Even the

poet, Jayant, in *Vyateet* (1954) does a stint as a commissioned army officer. He is the most explicit about renunciation as he takes sanyasa in the end. He is also the most sadistic because he has never felt love and Jainendra believes love alone can confer humanism. Women offer themselves unstintingly to him. It is he who spurns them: the poor and tormented Budhiya with kindness, and the rich and beautiful Chanderi with extreme cruelty. Renunciation or sanyasa is his atonement and writing the book *Vyateet* his confession. But most important is his realization, 'How could I, a sanyasi, escape from giving love?' In the end he says, 'Life seems a useless burden. Why could I never lose it in giving? Then I would have got something and not wandered like this. But there is another birth, that's all I hope for.'

As for Mrinal, readers have long been exercised by the questions: was Mrinal a masochist, bent upon self-laceration or was she an ascetic, full of love for the lowly and the poor, intent upon serving humanity? We may well ask—if her object was to serve humanity why did she opt to live with a boorish, uncultivated man? Had she no option? She certainly had. She was well educated and had worked as a teacher. It was her insistence on telling the unalloyed truth which got her in trouble each time. Modern rationalist readers insist that Mrinal was a masochist, who got into the habit of punishing herself because of the childhood trauma of being beaten by her sister-in-law for receiving a love letter. Others look upon her as a compassionate woman dedicated to service, a minor Mother Teresa.

In the author's world view we begin to see that the explanation is not quite so linear. The common thread running through Jainendra's novels is disillusionment with the hedonist urge. He felt that real freedom came from renunciation of all desires. Since an ascetic wants nothing, no one could exploit him. Since he had no desires, nothing could hold him in bondage. He was free forever of the dominance of material goods, the emotional hold of relationships and the dictates of society.

Looking at Mrinal from this standpoint, we have to concede that she was a woman of singular courage, who succeeded in discounting the mores practised by society. In the process, she obtained a sense of complete freedom. She sublimated personal renunciation by identifying with the poorest of the poor. She lived with them and served them, not from a sense of duty but as a fulfilling pursuit.

Love then is the moving force in Jainendra. Not in a physical sense between man and woman but as a manifestation of the divine. In the introduction to his first novel, *Parakh*, he says, 'Philosophy when it takes the form of a Shastra becomes totally cerebral. This special knowledge only divides the knower from the knowledge and does not let him taste oneness. Love alone can give the joyous taste of oneness; it alone gives the pain of separation. I give utmost importance to the torment of separation and pain of love in literature.'

Clearly for him, love meant pain and torment and the realization of a higher self through longing without physical consummation. He did not, however, eschew the adoration of the female body or the lure of money. But the ultimate goal was victory over both so the individual could merge willingly into other beings, society and finally God. Of profound significance is a sentence thrown out casually in typical Jainendra fashion in *Vyateet*, 'What freedom looked from afar, came close and it was wilderness.'

Jainendra has been both celebrated and attacked for his portrayal of women as guided by, what he called, feminine logic, 'Not irrational, only different and quite beyond the understanding of man' (*Vyateet*). With the advent of feminism came the concerted attack on his portrayal of self-lacerating women, willing to sacrifice their all for inferior men: with flashes of capricious aggressiveness in *Vyateet* and *Muktibodh* and the unabashed offer of the body to cure a disturbed revolutionary in *Sunita*. Interestingly, all of them were prompted by complex philosophical dictates, not by inner logic.

We may or may not agree with Jainendra's philosophy of renunciation and self-effacement. He would have been the first to concede that each individual was free to evolve his own philosophy and salvation. What I feel uncomfortable with is his putting the whole burden of it on women. As a result, none of his female characters—Mrinal in *Tyagpatra*, Neela in *Muktibodh*, Sunita in

Sunita, Ranjana in *Dashark*—are real people. They are there to act out the philosophy of the writer. As he delved deeper into its complex delineation, it imposed a tedious similarity on their characters. When Sunita disrobed herself followed by Hari Prassan's shocked withdrawal, remorse and renewed faith in life, it came as a clap of thunder, shattering the complacency of the literary world. But when Anita offered herself to Jayant later to ease his doubt and tension or when his wife Chanderi threw off her night dress in disgust at his indifference in *Vyateet*, it was just boring routine.

What appeals to my sense of the paradox is the manner in which Jainendra's woman revenged herself on those who rejected her. She penetrated their psyche deeply. It was easy for lesser men and women to imbibe the superficial devi image and gloss over the philosophy as too enigmatic, abstruse and secondary to creativity. It was also comforting to turn a blind eye to the weakness and cruelty of his men. After all, such fine women were willing to sacrifice themselves for them. Some men are born great; others are pushed to greatness by obdurate women bent upon negating themselves!

It had two repercussions on the portrayal of women in modern Hindi literature. First, even when women were depicted as independent, talented, ambitious and sexually liberated, they were shown to yearn for the life of an ordinary wife and mother. Second and more deleteriously, women were routinely subjected to sexual torment and abuse at home and work without the Jainendran freedom of choice. They were exploited because they could not defend themselves, not because they chose not to. The difference is crucial. For Jainendra, women are not the exploited or the weaker sex but the chosen one—chosen to work out the intricate and complex pattern of renunciation to finally merge in God.

Jainendra was attacked for his portrayal of the feminine mystique, and he was also attacked by Marxist critics ruling the Hindi literary world for choosing to deal with the individual without questioning the establishment or probing social malaise. Ironically, he was described by Premchand, the leading light of the Marxists, as the Maxim Gorky of Hindi. On the face of it, no two writers are more different than Jainendra and Maxim Gorky. Premchand, more astute than his followers, pierced through the false dichotomy between the individual and society and recognized the innate meeting of the two in Jainendra. The individual is shaped by society but not limited by it. The exploration of the possible expansion of limits is what literature is about. In Jainendra's words, 'Can a fish arrange for separate water for itself? If man draws oxygen from air for living, he gets oxygen of love from society. So I can't think how one can formulate a body of thought that pertains to the individual without society or to society without the individual.'

Without passion and empathy for the individual, literature would just be a treatise. A well researched treatise might have authenticity but it cannot match the intense effect of literature on the human psyche and sensibility. Nowhere is the dual relationship of the individual and society expressed more artistically and subtly than in *Tyagpatra*. When Mrinal asks Pramod to give money to help the poorest of the poor, it is not for charity but because he'll do 'good' to himself by giving his money away.

Jainendra's legacy lies in the courage of conviction and the ability to think for oneself, in the chiselling and honing of language to the sharpness of a rapier and, finally, in the integration of the two in an inseparable whole. If we read Jainendra in the context of his regimen of thought, we can exorcise the

ghost of unthinking acceptance of ideas. Each
can fashion an image of the self according to
his own perception.

To end with Jainendra's own words:

A writer lives more in the future
than in the present. He seeks the
welfare of the world, not to flatter it.
That is why society is compelled not
to understand him, to ignore him,
or at most to worship him—to be
scared of him. The world, because
it cannot comprehend him, cannot
love him. It is the misfortune of a
writer, or perhaps his good fortune,
that he is like a beacon . . . he does
not look to what society wants, but
the illness it suffers from. He seems
disinterested but he perceives the deep
anguish hidden in the depths of the
heart of society. He wants to create
a present which has the radiance of

its dreams. His connection to society is not of acceptance but also not of rejection. He is humble but unrelenting.

April 2011   Mridula Garg

New Delhi

ACKNOWLEDGEMENTS

My grateful thanks, first and foremost, to Shri Pradip Kumar, who generously gave me permission to translate Jainendra Kumar's novel.

My gratitude also to Dr Rupert Snell, who suggested this translation, and who is and remains mentor, guru, friend and guide; to Usha Bubna, for her patient reading of my translation, for her invaluable insights, and her constant support and encouragement; and to Vipasha Bansal, Piyali Sengupta and Urmi Sen for their suggestions and corrections.

Finally, my thanks to Sivapriya, my editor, who kept this together and to Ankita, who saw it through to the end.